*Dear Reader,*

When Erin O'Neill walked out of my life twelve years ago, I half expected her to keep her promise and come back to me after she finished school. I used to tease her about being a romantic, but maybe I let a little of it rub off on me when I began to believe that an uptown girl from the East would actually come back to a footloose young cowboy from a South Dakota Indian reservation.

Twelve years later she's back, thinking she'll risk her neck playing detective, and I'm thinking that's not *all* she'll be risking when she meets up with an older and wiser Hunter Brave Wolf. But one look into those soft, sad eyes of hers and I wasn't about to let anything hurt her again—including me.

Sincerely yours,

Hunter Brave Wolf

*South Dakota*

MEN MADE IN AMERICA

# KATHLEEN EAGLE
## *For Old Times' Sake*

*South Dakota*

Silhouette® Books

Published by Silhouette Books New York

**America's Publisher of Contemporary Romance**

For my daughter—
beautiful, brown-eyed Elizabeth Marie

**SILHOUETTE BOOKS**
300 East 42nd St., New York, N.Y. 10017

FOR OLD TIMES' SAKE

Copyright © 1986 by Kathleen Eagle

ISBN: 0-373-45191-1

Published Silhouette Books 1986, 1993

All the characters in this book have no existence outside the imagination of the author and have no relation whatsoever to anyone bearing the same name or names. They are not even distantly inspired by any individual known or unknown to the author, and all incidents are pure invention.

® and ™ are trademarks used under license. Trademarks recorded with ® are registered in the United States Patent and Trademark Office, the Canadian Trade Marks Office and in other countries.

**Printed in the U.S.A.**

# Chapter 1

One hundred and six degrees of high-plains heat had a way of eroding one's patience. Erin O'Neill passed her tongue over dry lips and turned her face from the hot wind in disgust. She'd forgotten how mercilessly this wind blew—a hot, dry echo in her ears. Arms folded firmly across her chest, she rounded the front of her red Toyota and marched from headlight to headlight. Then she tossed a swatch of yellow hair and let the wind carry it from her forehead as she eyed the young Indian sentinel at the roadblock.

The man shifted uncomfortably as he balanced himself on the top bar of the homemade tubular steel gate that stretched across the gravel road. Below his dangling moccasined feet, a spray-painted sign read No Admittance, and another proclaimed *Camp Wanbli we śa*. Crimson Eagle Camp. Two parts Lakota and one part English, Erin mused. Had she been in a dif-

ferent mood, she might have speculated on the significance of that combination, along with the sentinel's
uneasy balance. For now she left it at a straightforward observation.

He was probably eighteen or twenty, long and lean
in his faded denim jacket and jeans. A red bandanna
anchored shoulder-length black hair to his head, and
narrowly slitted eyes blocked the sun's glare. From his
protective perch he betrayed no interest in Erin's
presence. Everything at his back was his, and that was
that.

Erin saw a spiral of dust at the top of the distant
rise, and she shaded her eyes with her hand as she
willed this promise of an open gate to move quickly
down the gravel road. The cloud of dust became a vehicle, then a car, then a white car—small—much like
her own. The man on the fence didn't move until the
car slowed to a stop at his back. Then, like a cat
springing from a high place, he leaped to the ground
and unlocked the heavy chain. The gate whined as it
swung open, and the car moved closer to Erin.

Gravel crunched as the tires rolled to a stop. Erin's
pent-up energy carried her the first few steps, but then
the driver emerged, and she hesitated. He slammed his
door, and she stiffened. Twelve feet apart, across a
distance of a foot for every year they'd been apart,
Erin O'Neill and Hunter Brave Wolf eyed each other.

In Erin's mind a more rawboned Hunter gave her a
hard, quick kiss and drove a desperate warning into
her soul with young love's eyes. *You're coming back,
Erin. Don't forget that.* Ignoring the airport bustle, he
caught her close again for a longer, harder kiss. *Don't
forget this.*

"Hello, Erin. It's been a long time."

His voice was as she remembered—that strong, quiet timbre that had always caused her a kind of shortness of breath. That hadn't changed, either. His tongue gave her name a wind-in-the-trees sound. She took a long, steadying breath. "Hunter," she acknowledged. "I suppose I should be surprised, but I'm not."

"You mean, surprised to see me?" There was a hint of a smile on the generous mouth, but his dark, deep-set eyes held no expression. "Surely you remember what a small world it is out here, Erin. You were bound to see me sooner or later."

"Surprised to see you *here*, I mean." Her gesture indicated the series of surrounding hills—low hills in the front line, backed by large, deep-purple hills marching up from the rear. "Here in this...this activists' camp. I thought you..."

He shook his head, raising a silencing hand. "You thought little of me. I'm the one who should be surprised to see you, but I'm not. I'd heard you were here."

"Is this your little enterprise, Hunter? Are you in charge here?" If he were, she could use that as an irritant and maybe work up some disdain, which might make this easier in the long run. If she had to deal with *this* Hunter, it would be best if she could dislike him from the start—the better to forget the younger version and the way she'd felt whenever he'd turned those predatory eyes her way.

Again he shook his head, and the amusement was still evident, but only at the corners of his mouth. "Our old friend, Johnny Parker is more or less head honcho now that Ray Two Bows has been arrested. You remember Johnny.''

Johnny and Hunter and Erin. Another mental image flashed through her mind of a setting sun behind a hilltop cemetery, the big cross a black silhouette against the blazing orange sky, and three riders dashing to make curfew, taunting, daring one another and laughing into the wind. Erin smiled wistfully. Then she caught his knowing look and glanced over her shoulder at the sentinel, who'd taken up his post again.

"He says I can't go up there," Erin said, indicating the young man with a nod.

"Then you can't."

Her glistening green stare locked with Hunter's. His dark, steady gaze reflected his view that he considered this to be an obvious conclusion. The demanding spark in her eyes insisted that every lock had its key. "I told him to get someone down here who could let me in," she informed Hunter, her bearing that of one who was accustomed to commanding attention.

"This man could have let you in," Hunter pointed out. Why could she never see the obvious? "He didn't because you're not welcome here. You're a *wašicu*—a white woman."

*A* wašicu. *A white woman.* It had been a long while since she'd thought of herself in those terms. She looked up at Hunter's lean, angular face. The emotionless black eyes and the hollow-sounding words gave her a chill. Squaring her shoulders, she tossed the errant swatch of hair back from her face again.

"My sister died up there, Hunter. She was a white woman, too."

"That's exactly why they don't want you here. No one can guarantee your safety."

"Why not?" Erin bristled. "Is there a bounty on white women up there? My sister was murdered in this place six months ago, and I want to know why."

Hunter sighed, and the sigh softened his eyes. "We'd all like to know why. Louise was a good woman. She came to help. No one here wished her dead."

"Ah, but *someone* did, and someone got his wish, and I want to see where it happened and talk to the people who saw her last. They tell me about leads, investigations, arrests, but no one's been charged. No one's been tried for murdering my sister. I want some answers, Hunter."

"I have no answers for you. Far as I know, neither do they." He tossed his chin toward the hills, his eyes leaving hers only for a second.

"Why can't I ask them for myself? Why can't I see for myself where it happened?" Erin's voice was rising with emotion, and her throat was tight.

Hunter turned his thoughtful gaze to the horizon behind her. "Those people just want to be left alone. They don't need any more negative publicity."

Her reaction was immediate, arms stiffening at her sides, elbows locked in ramrod position. The hot flash in her eyes rocked him back slightly. "Negative publicity!" she spat. "Is that what my sister's death meant around here? Negative publicity? My God! Louise's death made a little ripple in your world, and you've given the ripple a name: *negative publicity*."

There was no warmth in his eyes, and Erin wasn't interested in the fatigue that pinched them at the corners as he spoke. "They wanted to make a statement. That's why they're camped up there on federal land in tents and makeshift shacks. They want the country to talk about treaties and the status of Indian claims. Instead, they're talking about FBI investigations and shootings."

"I'm sorry your little exposition didn't go as planned," she snapped, hanging an icicle on every syllable. "Perhaps next time you'll see that everyone knows his part and the guns are all loaded with blanks."

She'd lost her sister, Hunter reminded himself. It was her turn for bitterness, and no one could deny her the right. Twelve years ago Erin had come west on a lark—a college girl looking for a different way to spend her summer. At summer's end she'd gone back to her ivory tower with a carpetbag full of stories for her roommate, leaving Hunter an expert on the unlikelihood of fairy-tale endings. But Louise was a different story. She and her husband had been church workers, and they had come to Crimson Eagle not to make a political statement, but to offer a humanitarian contribution. It was the only kind of giving Hunter had come to admire.

"Look, Erin, this isn't *my* show. I'm a newspaper man. I observe and report. That's all."

"Report to me, then," she challenged. "Who shot my sister?"

He shook his head, the coarse, raven hair flip-flopping in the wind from one side of his bronze forehead to the other. "I'd like to know the answer to that. I've covered the investigation from step one. They know who they want to charge—people they'd like to put out of circulation. That's why they're not making any progress." There was soft menace in his voice and hard danger in his eyes. "I'd love to know who killed Louise, and I'd love to have five minutes alone with him before anyone else got to him."

"I'm touched. Unconvinced, but touched."

Suddenly he'd had enough of this. "It has nothing to do with the fact that she was your sister. It has to do with the fact of her goodness, her unselfishness. We lost a good friend. Your marching into that camp won't change that, so there's no point in your being here." Hunter thrust his hands into the front pockets of his jeans and rocked back a bit, eyeing her. "What you should do is go back to Connecticut and let the FBI earn its pay."

"You could get me in up there if you wanted to," she insisted.

He waited a moment for effect. "I don't want to."

"Then I'll find someone else," she returned.

"I'm sure you will. You have before."

That, of course, struck the mark dead center. She wouldn't try to top it. She turned quickly and returned to her car. Hunter's characteristically hooded eyes gave him a natural advantage in the bright South Dakota sunlight. He stood there watching, seemingly unconcerned, as Erin spun her steering wheel hand over hand and reversed the car, her bumper narrowly missing his shins as it arced past.

His hands were frozen in his pockets, his feet rooted where she'd left him standing, but his heart wouldn't take the hint. It longed after the car like a child left behind. His brain knew how pointless it was to protest his heart's making a fool of itself again. It had taken twelve years for his brain to assume its rightful executive role in the person of Hunter Brave Wolf, but now Erin O'Neill was back, and Hunter hadn't been prepared.

Abruptly stirring himself, Hunter reached his car in three long strides. He wasn't really sure what Tony Younghawk, still perched on the gate, said as Hunter jerked open the door and folded himself into the front seat, so he tossed a nod out the window in response to the casual salute of Tony's forefinger. Erin, of course, would be on her way to the mission, which would be on his way to McLaughlin, and so he had no choice but to follow.

He'd had no choice twelve years ago, either. He'd asked her to come back then—finish school and come back—and she'd promised she would. She hadn't, of course. She'd gone back to her world, where designers dictated the choice of everything from toothbrushes to tennis shoes, and where the well-bred lady wouldn't sound very convincing confessing to loving the untutored Indian cowboy. So she hadn't confessed. And she hadn't come back.

He was following her. She'd driven seventy miles before she saw the distant image in her rearview mirror. It could have been any white car, but it was his, and she knew it. He'd stayed well back, and she wondered when he'd learned to restrain the heavy foot that once put a battered blue pickup through impossible paces on hardpan prairie roads. Was this road paved with memories for him, too?

The white car drew closer. He was watching her now, and she knew what he must be thinking. Damn his eyes and damn his judgments. She'd been a coward, plain and simple. She hated this endless, branchless road for its lack of alternatives, and she cursed the treeless countryside for its lack of shelter. She felt like a rabbit darting across a fresh-plowed flat just ahead of the wolf. He was bearing down on her, and her soul was exposed to him, and he judged her—judged her as, damn him, *damn him*, he had every right to do. Her heart pounded, and she panicked at the unreasonable dread of being caught.

The railroad crossing sign barely registered itself on Erin's consciousness as she flicked a quick glance to one side. Her eyes met a hill. Returning her focus to the road ahead, she cranked up the volume on the radio and let an old Creedence Clearwater song drown everything else out, including the long low whistle the Burlington Northern gave as it rounded the bend between the two small hills and aimed for the crossing.

Wide-eyed, Hunter Brave Wolf couldn't believe what he was seeing. His stomach jacked itself into his throat just before he uttered a prayer, "My God, Erin, stop the car." Helplessly squeezing the steering wheel, he willed her to hit the brakes. She finally did, but in the seconds before the train reached her, he thought she'd waited too long. His heart stopped.

As if in fright, the Toyota's engine died as the car lurched to a stop, its bumper hovering near the tracks—over or just short, Erin didn't know which. *It's going to hit me.* She looked up at the train and saw the horror in the engineer's face before shutting her eyes in a desperate attempt to make everything go away. There was a jolt and a whoosh, and finally the droning whistle split her head from ear to ear. She opened her eyes again.

The train rolled past Erin's blank stare. Metal wheels clicking over smooth rails whispered, "ALmost got you ALmost got you ALmost got you...."

"What the hell were... Are you all right? You crazy... Hey! Are you okay?"

Dumbly Erin turned her face toward her left shoulder, which was being grabbed. Then she was a rag doll, plucked from a box by hands determined to shake her wrinkles out—and all the while she heard the retreating whisper "ALmost got you ALmost got you ALmost got you...."

"Erin, you're not hurt. Now, for God's sake, get your head on straight."

"I... almost got hit by a train," she managed in a childlike voice.

"Yeah, you did." His eyes rolled heavenward with relief as he kneaded her shoulders with his palms. "You *almost* got hit by a train. Nudged your bumper, in fact." With a nervous chuckle he added, "Damned good bumper you've got there."

"I didn't see it until..."

"Obviously. What in the hell were you doing?"

"Oh... Hunter... I..." Her face crumpled a little tighter with each word, and she sagged in his hands. "...didn't see..."

Her long-fingered, perfectly manicured hands trembled in front of her face, making a futile attempt to hide her wild-eyed terror. He moved instinctively to protect her with his body, surrounding her with himself and letting her sink against him.

"It was so close," she whispered to his collarbone. "It came...so close."

"I know. I saw it." The image of what he'd almost had to witness crashed through his brain and plummeted to his gut, and he gave his head a slight shake to clear it. "But an inch is as good as a mile, Erin. You're okay."

He felt her nod in the hollow of his neck, and he assumed the little mewling sound she made was some kind of assent, but her all-over trembling was disconcerting. He recalled the times when she'd trembled in his arms with better cause. The memory made him gather her closer—for old times' sake. And she, no doubt for old times' sake, as well, responded with a shaky sigh.

He didn't know how long he stood there holding her that way. Patience was part of his culture. Waiting was second nature, and time was not a factor. When she looked up at him with that prim face full of unshed tears he offered a grim smile. "Okay now?"

The smile she returned was tentative at best. "Sure. It missed me, right?"

"I guess we could say it *kissed* you. How did you like being kissed by a moving train?"

She shook her head, shivering as if she'd just surfaced in a cold lake. "I could *see* myself, Hunter. I watched myself shatter into a million pieces just before—"

"Before it went on by you. Hey!" The spark in his eyes gave his smile a new lilt as he surveyed her face. "Were you daydreaming at the wheel? Having kamikaze delusions or what?"

"I...uh..." Fidgeting at the sudden awareness of being in his arms, Erin glanced first to one side, then the other, her eyes leaping over his face. "I *looked*. The hill was...I guess I just didn't see..." Bracing herself with a firm grip on his forearms, she looked down at their feet—a couple of brown cowboy boots conversing with a couple of canvas deck shoes. "I don't know what I could have been thinking," she lied.

But of course he knew. "These roads can be hypnotic," he offered, catching her errant eyes and holding them with a dark, steady gaze. "Miles and miles of nothing, and then suddenly..."

His eyes were as she remembered—hot and predatory one minute, soft and liquid and endearing the next.

"Suddenly..." she murmured.

Her eyes were as he remembered—verdant, screening her thoughts, then turning cool and inviting.

"Suddenly...wham!" he growled.

"Suddenly wham..." she whispered. But the only sound was Erin's soft whimper as their lips found each other. They were responding to an instinct from the past, reaching to a long-stored need suddenly recalled. Their arms reacted instinctively, too, winding about each other quickly, reaching to satisfy the need.

Her hands sought the coarse thickness of his hair, and he clutched her tightly to himself, desperate for the impossible. He knew what he wanted, but he would not allow his brain to name it. His body knew it and burned with it. His hands knew it, and her cotton shirt would be rubbed off her back if they had their way. But his brain would not name the impossible.

They released each other all at once, as if signaled, and they stood back a pace and stared, both breathless. Finally Erin turned away, unsure of her bearings. Her car was directly at her back, and for some reason she'd forgotten it was even there. She stumbled as she turned, brought up short by the open car door. He caught her by the elbow, and she bobbled ungracefully.

"Where are you going?" The gravel in his voice betrayed his own emotion.

"I have to get back."

"I'll drive you. You've had quite a scare. I don't think you ought to be..."

"No, Hunter, I'm fine."

"You're disoriented. You're shaking like a leaf."

His hand slid from her elbow to her shoulder, and she knew he was trying to steady her, but somehow the trembling only intensified. *How do you like being kissed by a moving train?* Oh, God, I'm still alive. After all this time—after twelve long years—I'm still alive.

"Come on, I'll drive you," he repeated quietly.

"My car..."

"We'll drive your car. I'll lock mine up and come back for it later. We're not too far from McLaughlin." She looked back up at him, her eyes full of gratitude, as though he'd just awakened her from a terrible nightmare. He wanted to kiss her again, softly this time. Instead he smiled and said, "Come on. I'll buy you a drink to steady your nerves."

"I think if I just had a little time to calm down . . . and maybe a cup of tea . . ." Her slight smile was apologetic.

"Tea and time. Easy order to fill. I'll move my car off the road. You climb into yours."

Erin wanted to be swallowed up in the bucket seat. Though she'd have preferred an armored truck or a tank, she'd settle for any protective enclosure. She wanted safety. The click of the seat belt gave her small comfort.

At the sound Hunter swung a smile her way. "Don't worry. I take it easy nowadays. Saves on gas and fines."

"Funny, isn't it?" she mused. "I used to accuse you of driving like a maniac, and I'm the one who almost ran into a train."

He saw himself behind the wheel of a battered blue pickup, careering across the prairie with a young green-eyed woman at his side. The more she shrank down in the seat, the faster he drove. Suddenly he veered off the gravel road and onto the rutted hardpan. He grinned when she bounced hard in the seat and shrieked, "Please, Hunter, slow down!"

"Funny," he echoed. "The irony is funny, I guess." He kept a steady eye on the road ahead. "How long will you be staying?"

"I don't know. As long as it takes. I'm staying at the mission, and Marlys has already put me to work in the kitchen. They're having some sort of conference this weekend. She says I can hire on as a full-time priest's wife's helper, but I'm sure the pay—"

"What does 'as long as it takes' mean?" he injected quietly.

"I want to know what happened to Louise."

The glance he flickered at her didn't lack sympathy, but it showed his disapproval. "Your sister was shot to death by an unknown assailant. It happened in the dead of night in a camp full of 'Indian activists,' many of whom were armed. A nineteen-year-old boy was questioned and later released. The next suspect was an Indian activist who's been a thorn in a lot of people's sides, and then a particularly vocal young Indian woman, but there wasn't a shred of evidence against anyone. The investigation continues, but the trail, as they say, is stone cold." He shrugged. "That's it."

"I knew all that," Erin said. "That isn't enough. That doesn't tell me why."

"We may never know why." Hunter scanned the jagged horizon, where flat-topped buttes met the sky like a castle wall. "Even if they find the person who pulled the trigger, we may never really know why Louise died, Erin. And even if there is a reason, it's probably one that means something for us and has nothing to do with you or Louise." He turned his hard, level gaze on Erin. "Your sister will still be dead. They can hang the whole damned camp, and Louise won't be any less dead."

Erin was in no mood to argue. She turned her face to the side window and remembered Louise's enthusiasm for life. She was struck by the absurdity of the idea that such vigor could be so quickly snuffed out. She hardly knew she'd voiced her thoughts until she heard his echo.

"Yes, she had a good heart," Hunter confirmed.

"She was in high school when I came here as a summer volunteer twelve years ago. She thought it was so *noble* then, but later she outgrew all the romantic notions. She came and she stayed to work for the church...simply because it was right for her to."

"She took food and clothing up to the camp, transported children, built outhouses—you name it," Hunter recalled.

The question seared her mind, and again she thought out loud. "Did she die for anything, Hunter?"

He shook his head. "I can't answer for another person's death. But I know she lived for something. There was never any doubt of that."

Erin nodded. She wanted the same to be said of her someday. After all was said and done, to know she'd lived for something. And then she saw once again the horror in the engineer's face. She shuddered.

She found herself watching Hunter's hands control the car. She'd loved his hands. Back in the days when she'd loved every part of him, she'd especially loved to watch his hands—dusky brown and square, with long fingers and neatly trimmed nails. Watching them gave her a sense of security. They moved with assurance—never hurried, never any wasted motion. She remembered peering between two weathered gray fence slats to watch those steady hands check the rigging on a high-headed bareback bronc. The very thought of his getting up on those wild-eyed horses had always terrified her, but there was something reassuring in the way his hands moved over the equipment, seeing that all the straps were tight, the buckles fast.

Hunter turned the steering wheel and pitched the little car over the hump of a paved driveway. At a glance Erin took in the red brick, green shrubbery and fastidious white trim, and wondered aloud, "Where are we?"

"My house," Hunter informed her, stopping the car. He noted a little feeling of satisfaction as he said it, and he felt silly. His apartment in L.A. might have impressed her, but not this house on the edge of a little prairie town in the middle of a reservation. He knew this woman could never appreciate what he had here. He remembered a time when he'd had nothing but dreams to impress her with, and they hadn't done the trick. How often he'd wondered since whether it would have made any difference if he'd had something he could point to, as he did now. He gestured to a second building and said, "And that's my business."

Erin cut a sharp glance in his direction, bristling at the crude quip, but when she followed the direction of his nod, she realized he meant the comment literally. The steel-sided gray building, sitting a quarter of a mile up the road from the house, was identified by a no-nonsense black-and-white sign as Brave Wolf Publishing.

"It's a new building, isn't it?" she remarked. "I remember that drive-in on the hill beyond it and the gas station, but that building wasn't there twelve years ago."

"It wasn't there three years ago. I built the business from the ground up, you might say. Come on in." He leaned out the car door, adding, "Ignore the dog. She hates company."

Expecting something large and predatory, Erin stepped over the threshold to be held at bay by a feisty blond terrier. The dog yapped hysterically until Hunter stepped in and hissed at it. After a few seconds' quiet Hunter called, "C'mon, Blondie," and laughed when the dog jumped happily into his arms.

"The spoils from a defunct relationship," Hunter explained, leading the way toward the kitchen, the dog lapping his chin. "She got the apartment, since it was her deposit on the lease, and I got the dog."

The information registered with a sharp stab in Erin's chest. Until now she'd thought of the past twelve years only in terms of her failure to keep her promise and the sadness that had followed. Had she assumed that Hunter had been trapped in a depression of his own? Had she thought he'd been biding his time for twelve years? "Your apartment?" she responded, surveying the sand-and-clay-toned living room as she followed him through it. "Where was that?"

"In L.A. I lived in L.A. for seven or eight years. That's where I learned . . . Never mind. You want tea? Let's see . . ." The neatly organized cabinet yielded a box of tea bags. Hunter turned, dog in one arm, tea in the other hand, which was raised in triumph. "You got it. How about boiling some water? Part of the treatment here is to keep you busy, take your mind off the cause of the trauma."

Erin complied, accepting the small pan he handed her. She turned the faucet on full force, splashing a small geyser of water up in her face. Fumbling with the faucet, she dropped the pan with a clatter and a disgusted, "Oh . . . tsk!"

Hunter's hand closed over hers, and he helped her shut the water off. With his other hand he caught her chin and turned her face toward him. His smile was tight-lipped, almost regretful, as he wiped a drop of water from her chin with his thumb. "Oh, tsk," he echoed. "Still the lady, no matter what. Let me hear you say damn, Erin. Just once."

She didn't know if she could say anything when he stood this close. It had always melted her insides when he touched her like this, with a hand that seemed too big to be so gentle. "If that train had hit me, you'd have heard some curses," she promised at last. "I can't stop shaking, and I feel like a fool. I just wasn't thinking."

"Oh, I think you were," he said quietly. "I know I was. Thinking how much you still looked like the Erin O'Neill I used to know, and how little. You don't look like you're made of porcelain anymore. Your face has more character." He touched the tiny lines at the corner of her eye. "More cares, I guess. What were you thinking, Erin?"

He pulled his hands back slowly, but his eyes mesmerized her, and there was no answer but the truth. "Wondering what you must think of me."

"You mean after all this time?" She nodded. "The memories come flooding back, don't they?" This time she raised her brow in resigned assent. "Mostly the good ones. The nice ones. I used up the resentment a long time ago."

"Used it up?"

Turning to the sink and filling the pan himself, he explained. "I built up a real head of steam on it. Left the reservation, went back to school, got a good job.

Guess I showed you, huh?'' His dark eyes laughed at
the notion as he walked around her to the stove.

"I never doubted—"

"Never doubted that what talents I had weren't
salable. For overseeing the mission's little cattle op-
eration I was making a hundred and fifty dollars a
month plus room and board, and then whatever I
could pick up at the local jackpot rodeos. If you'd
been my daughter, I'd have locked you back up in the
tower and swallowed the key to keep you away from a
guy like that.''

"It was my own decision in the end," she admitted
quietly.

"And a wise one. I was surprised to hear you were
Erin O'Neill again. What was your married name?''

"Bates." Her voice sounded distant and hollow, and
she glanced uneasily out the window over the sink.

"Erin Bates? That *is* lackluster. Erin O'Neill is
much better. It always reminded me of Scarlett
O'Hara."

Erin found she could laugh, at least a little. "Scarlett would have shaken her fist at that train and been
on her way as soon as it passed."

His voice shifted to a serious tone. "Scarlett would
be out to avenge her sister's death, too."

"I don't want revenge," she assured him. "I want
justice."

His chuckle held a sardonic edge. "Don't we all."
He handed her a mug from the cupboard and took
another one down for himself. "This may be the time
Erin O'Neill learns that we don't always get what we
think we have coming to us. Justice can be hard to
come by around here."

"I'm going to try," she insisted. "Shouldn't you do something about getting your car? If anything happens to it..."

"You'll feel just terrible," he finished for her with a smile. "I'm going to make a call. Find a comfortable chair in the living room and try a few relaxation exercises or something."

Moments later he joined her on the overstuffed sofa, announcing that a friend would be along soon to give him a ride back to get his car, and she was to take it easy until he returned. He suggested that they might have some supper. The sound of a car pulling up in the driveway brought him to his feet. He glanced out the front window and then back to Erin, whom he found standing behind him. He hadn't managed to put her at ease yet. "I'll be back shortly. Help yourself to more tea, and just take it easy."

She glanced down at the ceramic mug in her hand and nodded. Without looking up, she felt him move toward the door, then hesitate. "Erin," he began, and she raised her chin in his direction. "The kiss was just for old times' sake. Don't let it bother you." The parting wink he gave her was a gesture that seemed too familiar to be a twelve-year-old memory. Her stomach fluttered as he shut the door behind him.

Moving closer to the window, Erin let the open drape shield her from his view. A smiling blonde moved to the passenger's seat of a white van, which had Brave Wolf Publishing painted in black on the door. Hunter took the wheel, backing the van down his driveway.

*Don't let it bother you.* The close call with a train had bothered her. But, yes, the kiss had shaken her, too. She'd been hit by a right-left combination, and she was reeling.

Erin set the mug on the counter, noticing the words, You're the Boss, Baby on the side of it. She decided not to be there when Hunter returned. For old times' sake.

# Chapter 2

The mission's buildings were pristine white in the morning sun. Erin squinted at the sky, then slid a pair of sunglasses on. The sky was everything here, a great blue bowl overturned on a plate, and the air was clear and pure. She could have done with a few more trees, but she couldn't ask for better air or more sky.

Following the narrow sidewalk from the girls' dorm, where she'd been given the counselor's apartment, Erin wondered that any time at all had passed since she'd taken this path to breakfast every morning. The swatch of hair she hitched behind her ear had been much longer then, and straighter, and she'd worn jeans and a T-shirt rather than the crisp green slacks and short-sleeved cotton blouse she wore this morning. The only sounds today were the flapping of Erin's sandals against her heels and the chirping of small birds as they jostled for perches in the precious few cottonwoods.

There had been more noise back then. Three other young college women, half a dozen teenagers and several younger children had converged on the dining hall three times a day, laughing and chattering, playing a little pinch-and-dodge on the way in. The children were gone now. The church had closed its boarding school, and the handful of children who used to stay on through the summer with Father Wilkins and his wife, Marlys, had found other places to go. The absence of children's voices left an empty quiet hanging over the mission, which had been a landmark in this part of South Dakota for decades.

From the landing of the split-entry dining hall Erin heard a soft murmur of voices, which quieted when a man launched into the agenda for the day's conference. The Reverend Carter Wilkins had a deep, resonant "pulpit" voice. On a clear summer Sunday morning his sermon could be heard from the cemetery on the hill, half a mile away. That was the way to "have it all—sermon and sky together," she remembered Hunter telling her once as they lay in the grass and watched the clouds drift overhead.

As she slipped down the stairs and into the kitchen hallway Erin almost expected to see Hunter washing up at the bathroom sink. He would have started his chores before breakfast, and he'd be starving. He'd look up from a towel and give her a slow, lazy grin.

A woman greeted her instead. "Good morning, sunshine. Breakfast is over, but I saved you a plate." Marlys Wilkins was ten years Erin's senior and a full head shorter. With short black hair, bronze skin and one of those petite figures that made a tall woman like Erin feel bulky, Marlys was an inexhaustible source of energy. She always had "Yes, let's do it," written all over her face.

"I'm sorry I slept in," Erin said, accepting the cup of coffee Marlys handed her. "I wanted to help you with this."

"And you will. Twenty-three for lunch." Marlys closed the pass-through window over the counter between the kitchen and dining room, set a stool by the counter and indicated that Erin should sit. "I'm anxious to hear about that wild-goose chase you went on yesterday. Did they let you past the gate?"

"No."

With a triumphant clatter Marlys set a plate of scrambled eggs, bacon and a caramel roll the size of a man's fist on the counter. "I told you you wouldn't be able to get in there. If they'd let *me* in, I'd go up there and *really* cuss that Johnny Parker out. They arrested Ray Two Bows for inciting a riot or some such thing, and that should have been the end of it. They all should have gone home." She shook her head. "Poor Louise. We never thought there'd be any violence up there, Erin, not like that." Pulling up a stool, Marlys gave the younger woman a curious look. "You got a black eye or something?"

"Hmm?" Erin responded through a sticky mouthful of roll.

"What's with the glasses?"

"Oh." With her free hand she lowered the dark glasses from her face. "I forgot. You know I can't go outside for the newspaper without—"

"And what's with the puffy eyes? What happened?"

The puffy eyes lowered. "Hunter was there."

And there it was, much to Erin's surprise. Asked what had happened, the first thing that came to mind wasn't not being able to get into the camp or the train nearly hitting her. She hadn't come directly back to the mission after leaving Hunter's house. She hadn't wanted to answer any questions just then, confused and shaken as she was. Instead she'd driven thirty miles to the small off-reservation town of Mobridge and had supper in a café. Then she'd gone to a movie, the title of which escaped her at the moment. When she thought she'd distracted herself sufficiently she'd driven back to the mission, put herself to bed and lain there with a crowd of pictures in her mind that could only be washed away by hot tears. And at the root of it all, Hunter was there.

Marlys gave her a knowing look. "Well, I didn't know he'd be there, but I told you you'd run into him sooner or later. How did he act? Did you two get into it?"

Erin shook her head. "I asked him to help me get past the gate, but he refused. Other than that, he was perfectly..." Carefully Erin set the caramel roll back on her plate and stared down at it before raising her eyes to let Marlys see her distress. "Oh, Marlys, I had a terrible scare. A train was coming, and I almost didn't stop in time. Hunter drove up behind me—saw the whole stupid thing. He took me to his house, and we..."

Marlys waited as long as she could before asking, "You what?"

Erin's innocent shrug reminded Marlys of the girl-woman Erin had once been. "We talked and had tea. He doesn't seem to hate me the way I expected him to. He treated me very kindly, like an old friend." Almost like an old friend, she thought. Remembering his kiss, she ran her tongue over her lips, as though there might be some trace left. And then she remembered the blonde in the van. "But then, why wouldn't he? So much time has passed, and we've both . . . changed."

"Of course you've changed. You were, what, nineteen? Twenty?" Marlys smiled the smile of someone who was thinking back on warm summer nights and couples holding hands. Dreamy-eyed, she remembered. "Carter was a summer volunteer, too, you know. He came back five years later as a priest of the Episcopal Church. He surprised a lot of people when he married a local Indian girl. Few people knew that I'd loved him when I was fifteen years old, when he came to that window three times a day for three whole months, and I was back there helping my mother with the cooking."

"Did he know?" Erin wondered.

"He must have suspected. I served him bigger portions than I gave anybody else."

"You still do," Erin laughed.

"And he's still as thin as a sapling, that man," Marlys said with a shake of her head. "You know, Erin, Carter and I have watched so many volunteers come and go over the years. We could always tell which ones would come back. This place seems to get under some people's skin, and they come back to work, maybe just for a year or two, maybe for good. We could always tell which ones they'd be."

"Did you think I'd come back?"

"We *knew* you would." Marlys's dark eyes danced Erin's way. "It just took you a little longer than we expected."

"But I'm not really *back*, not to stay. I'm just here because . . . I owe it to Louise."

"Nonsense. Louise is dead. All debts are canceled. And there's one thing you learn fast out here in Indian country: you don't go sticking your nose in other people's business."

Erin's green eyes flashed with surprise. "My sister's death *is* my business."

"But finding out who did it isn't. You don't want to get mixed up with those outlaws, Erin."

"The church did. Louise did."

Marlys sighed. "My husband and I don't always agree on the politics of these things. Some church groups collected food and clothing, and Louise was among those who transported supplies. The church does not officially support that kind of activity. Privately Carter and some others simply saw people in need and offered help."

"Louise could never turn her back on anyone who needed help," Erin mused. "What do you think of all this, Marlys?"

"The camp, you mean? It's a publicity stunt, as far as I'm concerned. But then, so were all the civil rights marches, and people died for those, too." Marlys shook her head over the way things had to be. "But publicity is Hunter's business, and murder is police business." She wagged a motherly finger in Erin's face. "You have no business up there." The finger came down, and there was mischief in Marlys's eyes. "Unless your business was with Hunter."

"I didn't expect him to be there." The mischief was still there, and Erin bristled slightly. "I'm not here to see Hunter."

"Doesn't matter much now, does it? You've seen him, and from the looks of your face, it shook you up more than a little."

"Nearly colliding with a train shook me up more than a little," Erin insisted.

"How did he seem to you, Erin?" Marlys wondered, ignoring Erin's remark. "How much has he changed?"

"I don't know. In some ways, not very much. But I certainly never expected him to become a newspaperman."

"What did you expect him to become?"

Marlys had never been one to sidestep an issue, Erin thought. "I don't know," she repeated, and she knew her voice had quavered like a child's. She cleared her throat and told herself to be truthful with her friend. "A rider of painted ponies, I guess. A dreamer of beautiful dreams."

"Beautiful dreams don't buy a house with a two-car garage," Marlys supplied.

"No, they don't." Erin remembered the big colonial she'd lived in with Arthur. "But you don't build a marriage without dreams." She glanced into Marlys's warm brown eyes and felt the need to say more. "The man I married didn't dream. He had plans for himself, and he had plans for me. Blueprints, in fact. He provided all the materials. All I had to do was follow directions, put the pieces together. It was a disas-

ter right from the beginning. I don't know why we
didn't recognize it sooner."

"No children?" Marlys asked.

"No children." Thank God, she thought. Arthur
had put in an order for two of them, no more, no
fewer, and he had begun to draw up the blueprints.
The sterility of the whole plan had, probably more
than anything else, forced Erin to admit that she was
suffocating as Mrs. Arthur Bates.

Marlys took Erin's dishes and handed Erin a par-
ing knife, directing her toward a pile of potatoes.
"You were right about Hunter," Marlys said. "He
dreams big. Not big bucks, but big ideals. And some
of the broncs he rides nowadays buck harder than the
rodeo stock ever did. I guess he was a pretty big-time
reporter out in L.A. Then some relative from some
reservation out in Montana died, and Hunter came
into some oil-lease land. He decided we were going to
have an independent, Indian-owned newspaper
around here, and I thought he was going to dash his
brains out against the brick wall called 'resistance to
change' getting it started. But he did it. He's forever
printing something to set somebody's teeth on edge,
and somebody's always threatening to sue him, but
everybody reads that paper. And it's brought about
some changes that were a long time in coming."

"Louise always tiptoed around Hunter in her letters," Erin remembered. "I knew he'd come back
home. When I asked how he was, she just said he was
fine. I envied Louise. She got such satisfaction out of
what she was doing." And because she was here, Erin
added mentally, *where I wanted to be.*

Marlys dried her hands on a length of white towel-
ing and considered Erin for a moment before offering
the suggestion she'd been mulling over since Erin's
arrival. "There's something you could do for me while
you're here, and I think you might get that same kind
of satisfaction out of it—knowing you helped get
something started." Erin raised a questioning brow,
and Marlys leaned closer, her brown eyes bright with
excitement. "I want to get a woman's project going
here at the mission, but I have to get the people at this
conference to back me on it. The last time I suggested
something like this, they told me I would need professional staff, and we couldn't afford that." With a
flourish Marlys gestured toward Erin. "You, my dear,
are the professional staff."

Erin's eyes widened. "But I'm a social worker!"

"Exactly."

"What would you want with a social worker? I
haven't had a job in years, which is why I'm unemployed at the moment."

"An unemployed social worker is just what I need.
You need the job so desperately that you'll work for
church wages, right?"

"I've been looking for something with a little
more..."

Marlys gripped Erin's shoulder. "You've been
looking for *something*, and you came here, Erin.
What you're looking for may be here."

"I don't intend to stay much longer."

Marlys smiled. "We go by Indian time. You're here
when you're here, and you'll go when it's right."

Carter Wilkins's red beard flashed in the kitchen
doorway. He raised unruly eyebrows, realizing he'd

interrupted a serious discussion, and offered a wide, white smile at the feminine faces turned his way. "You're on, Mrs. Wilkins. They seem to be in a pretty good mood. Did you, uh..."

Marlys nodded. "We've talked."

"And?" Carter prompted.

Marlys gave Erin's shoulder another squeeze before she joined Carter at the doorway. "She hasn't given me an answer yet."

Erin responded at the same time as Carter.

"Marlys, you know they won't consider..."

"Marlys, you haven't even told me..."

Marlys's brown eyes danced Erin's way. "Erin will give me her answer when she's ready. Come," she urged with a quick wave of her hand. "I could use some moral support."

Erin stood against the wall in the dining hall and listened to Marlys's presentation. The audience, Erin noted, was predominately male, a mix of brown and white faces, some with clerical collars, all absorbed in Marlys's sincerity. She proposed that the mission outfit one of its buildings for a craft center, invest in materials and provide an undisturbed space where traditional crafts, particularly quilting and beadwork, might be done. The work could be marketed nationally through catalogs. The center would reinvest in supplies and control quality, and the crafters would get a decent price for their work. Marlys offered examples of similar marketing projects in Appalachia and handed out sample catalogs. Several women who were well-known for their fine handiwork spoke of the need for such a center and of the difficulty they had in finding buyers locally.

Just as Erin was asking herself where a social worker might fit into this plan, Marlys answered the question. In addition to the craft center Marlys proposed to offer a "safe house," a retreat for women who were mistreated at home. The program would involve sheltering women and perhaps their children on a short-term basis. Here they would be safe, and in safety they would have time to seek counseling and legal action if they chose. Hearing the word "counseling," Erin unfolded her arms and straightened her shoulders.

Marlys let the group buzz among themselves for a moment. They were chewing on her plan, but she was ready for their indigestion. She knew Erin wouldn't let her down. Erin had come back, and she would do what needed to be done now.

"Are you proposing to add this assignment to Father Wilkins's workload?" came the first challenge.

"No one knows what that workload is better than I do," Marlys answered. "He would be only one of our counselors. I believe we'd need a social worker on staff, as well."

"Wait a minute, Marlys," cautioned a balding man with a collar. "You're talking real money now. Where are you going to get a social worker who wants to work at a mission? They're used to getting paid in U.S. currency."

Marlys sought Erin's eyes over the undercurrent of chuckles and the sea of shaking heads. The offer was out before the words had formed in Erin's brain. "I've agreed to work with Marlys to get this project under way."

Heads turned, and someone asked, "Who are you?"

"I'm your social worker" was the answer.

The conference was over, and the participants had gone away smiling. Marlys was a gem, they said, a real inspiration, even to the faithful. They didn't worry about how long Erin would stay. They were mission workers. They accepted each day's blessings and trusted there would be more tomorrow, or, if not tomorrow, then maybe the next day.

For Erin, tomorrow was a reality that should be faced in advance if possible. She hadn't promised that much, she told herself as she wandered aimlessly through the tall grass at the top of the bluff overlooking the river. She'd said she would help get this started, and they had been satisfied. How long would it take? A month? Two? She couldn't guess, since she really had no idea what she'd gotten herself into. She had some ideas, though. Lifting her face to the cool early evening breeze, she gazed across the river and smiled to herself. She had lots of ideas. It was an exciting project, and she would be one of the designers.

Without thinking about it she had passed the mission's main buildings—its two dorms, laundry, gym, dining hall, priest's house and the quaint old church—and now she found herself climbing the rails of the corral near the big red barn out back. A single horse pricked its ears and swung its head in Erin's direction.

This wasn't a mission horse, Erin decided, recalling the old mission mare, who'd once taken a bite out of the seat of her blue jeans. No, this stout bay reminded her of one Hunter had had. In fact, the first time she'd seen Hunter, standing here in this corral, he'd been working that horse. She remembered his bright-red Western shirt and faded jeans, and she remembered the predatory look he'd given her, and then the slow smile and the "Howdy, miss," that he always used to disarm the girls. It had certainly worked on Erin O'Neill.

Hoofbeats in the distance caught the bay's ears and Erin's, too, and both heads turned in the rider's direction. Erin knew him before she could see his face. She'd seen his body move that way with a horse so many times, in a liquid rhythm that gave her a deep warm feeling as she watched. His straw cowboy hat was pulled low on his forehead, and his denim jacket flapped behind him in time with the horse's trot. Erin climbed higher on the rails, admittedly hoping he'd see her.

And he did. She reminded him of one of those beautifully carved mastheads on the bow of an old ship as she leaned slightly forward over the top rail. The wind caught her white jacket like a sail, and her wheat-colored hair blew back from the face that could have been his homing beacon. Forgetting his routine of heading home at a walk, he turned the horse in Erin's direction and gave him his head.

It must have been simply a remembered courtesy, Erin thought later, because without any instruction she hopped over the rail and hurried to open the gate on the other side of the corral for him. He rode by her, and her nose welcomed the smell of horse sweat and leather. Hunter smiled down at her, his big sorrel mount prancing underneath him. "Howdy, miss."

Erin laughed. "I can't believe you said that!"

"Why not? They say it on TV. I used to get some cute blushes with just that one line." He leaned forward over the saddle horn and stretched his legs, nodding at her feet. "See you've got some boots on. Still like to ride bareback?"

"I haven't done a lot of riding lately," she confessed.

"Bet you can't even haul yourself up anymore," he challenged with a cocky, one-sided smile.

"Up where?"

He jerked his chin toward the unsaddled bay.

"I may not have ridden much lately, but I haven't exactly gone to pot," she pointed out, sizing up the bay from the ground.

"Didn't say you had. I need to walk this guy, cool him down. There's a bridle hanging in there on the wall. Think you remember how one works?"

"Of course I do." Erin found the bridle quickly and approached the bay with caution.

"He'll let you walk up to him. Ho, there, Gambler."

Erin settled the bit in the horse's mouth and slipped the split-ear headstall in place. "This is Gambler?" she asked. "How have you held on to him with all the moving you've done?"

"I sold him when I left. Bought him back."

"For old times' sake?" she wondered aloud as she got a good grip on the horse's withers with her left hand. This wouldn't be easy. She flexed her knees, tried a little experimental hop and repositioned her hands.

A low chuckle near her ear brought her head around. Hunter had dismounted and was standing disconcertingly close. The brim of his hat shaded them both from the slanted rays of the evening sun, and his smile was in his eyes. "Yeah," he said as he leaned down. "For old times' sake." Erin swallowed her surprise when he grasped her leg at the knee and ankle and said, "On three."

On the count of three she levered herself over the horse's back with a good deal of help from below. "I *used* to be able to do this," she reminded him with a grunt.

"I know." He took a step back to get a better view as she fitted her bottom into the curve of the horse's back. "I used to watch you do it."

She shot him an indignant look, and he laughed.

"I'll bet *you* can't haul *yourself* up there without using the stirrup anymore." She gave him a smug little grin.

Hunter hooked his left hand around the saddle horn, stepped back a little nearer the horse's head, and then swung himself off the ground and into the saddle with effortless grace. The feat brought a cheer from Erin. "What were we betting?" he asked with an irrepressible grin.

"Gentlemen's bet," she answered, nudging Gambler toward the gate with a tapping heel.

"That's two you've lost."

"Guess I'm no gentleman," was the cheery comeback.

"I think I just gave myself a hernia proving I am," he muttered, letting his horse follow. "I'll give you the best of five. Bet you can't beat me to the cemetery with a head start."

"Bareback? Not on your life! I'll be lucky if I can walk tomorrow."

He rose up beside her and tossed her a wink. "Next time, then."

A little sigh of relief escaped Erin's chest. She'd almost expected him to take off at a dead run, leaving her to try to hold her horse back or follow suit. There'd been a time when he would have.

The sun sank below the low-lying western hills, and the horses ambled across the stretch of spiky thistle and tufts of grass between the corrals and the cemetery. "Why do you keep your horses here instead of in McLaughlin?" Erin wondered.

"I keep them here by the padre's invitation," Hunter explained. "I think it's his way of luring me into the vicinity of the church."

"And has it worked?"

"I go once in a while, when I come down to ride on Sundays." He cocked his head and shrugged a shoulder. "More often than I used to. I guess this whole place is church to me—the mission, the river, those hills and draws. I know every nook and cranny where a calf can hide out here." He scanned the rise ahead. "When I was a kid we used to come to church with a team and wagon." Her look of surprise didn't escape him. "Yeah. A team and wagon. When you think about it, that wasn't so long ago. Church was a whole-day affair then, with a lot of visiting and singing and kids racing around the yard. And then there was dinner in the church basement. We've lost a lot of that. Whose fault do you think that is? Henry Ford's?"

"Partly," Erin judged. "But his invention must've been a late arrival out here if you can remember horse and buggy days."

"I remember teams and wagons, kerosene lamps and tubs and washboards," he recited, patting his mount's neck as though the horse might share in the memories.

"You never talked about those things . . . before."

"I was too young to appreciate good memories then." His smile told her how much he'd learned. "Besides, you were the girl from Connecticut whose daddy drove a T-bird. I wasn't about to tell you stories about the family buckboard."

She smiled and then lowered her eyes on the next thought. "You never told me you wanted to be a newspaperman, either."

"I hadn't thought of it yet. I didn't know what I wanted then." But I wanted you. I knew that much.

"When did you think of it?"

"When I went back to school. Went out to Montana, got a job as a ranch hand. I've got some relatives out there. I'd had about a year and a half of college. One day I just decided to go back. Found out I liked journalism."

They were skirting the cemetery now in a slow circle—the pace of riders more caught up in conversation than in exercising their horses. "What made you decide to go to Los Angeles?" Erin asked.

He grinned. "Got relatives out there, too. And I had a professor who knew somebody at the *Times*." he scanned the horizon below the pink-and-gray-streaked sky, and the grin faded. "Next question is, why did I come back?" He nodded thoughtfully and clicked his tongue. "That, Erin O'Neill, is a very good question. I ask it myself at least once a day. It sure as hell wasn't to get rich and famous; I can tell you that."

"Isn't your business—" she hesitated, hoping she wasn't hitting a sore spot "—profitable?"

"That depends on how you define 'profitable.'" Hunter tightened the reins, and the sorrel settled all four legs into a halt. Gambler took a few steps and then followed suit as Erin turned him to put the horses head to head. With one forearm draped over the saddle horn, Hunter leaned forward, sliding his other hand along his thigh as he considered Erin's face. "What would you consider to be a successful profit margin?"

Gambler shifted his weight under her as she hedged. "I don't know much about the publishing business."

"What kind of profit do you think a man has to make before he can consider himself successful?"

Erin measured her answer. "Whatever he needs, I guess, to live the kind of life that makes him happy."

Hunter registered that thought with a funny smile, then swung himself out of the saddle. Flicking the knotted reins over the horse's head, he said, "Then my business is profitable." He rubbed Gambler's neck, then looked up at his rider. "How's it going bareback?"

Her knees relaxed at the question. The fuzzy warmth of the horse's hide felt good under her, but it had been a long time. She wasn't sure she could dismount smoothly, much as she wanted to show Hunter she could.

He grinned up at her. "Wanna get down for a while?" They eyed each other for a moment, and then, with a hand at her waist, he offered to help. She arced her right leg over the horse's head and let herself slide over the curve of his side and into Hunter's hands. With her hands on his shoulders and his at her waist, Erin braced herself against the butterflies and refused to raise her chin. There was a cool breeze at her back and a deliciously warm one on her forehead.

"You dropped the reins," he said quietly.

"What?"

"Never let go of the reins when you dismount. I thought I taught you that a long time ago." His hand came away from her waist to reach behind him for Gambler's loose reins, which he tucked into her hand with a chuckle.

The horses followed as the couple shuffled leisurely through the tall grass. It was the kind of evening they'd loved to share, the quiet time when they could go off alone and talk and tease and share their dreams. It was a good time, Hunter thought, to be honest about important things.

"I started the business because I believe we need our own free press. We have a community here, with its own government, and a newspaper is a necessity. Not a paper that's subsidized and run by the government—I'm talking about an independently owned free press. Of course, a weekly newspaper serving a reservation isn't exactly a sound economic proposition, so I started a printing business."

"A printing business?"

"We have our own press—something most small-town newspapers can't afford. We print a number of other local newspapers, as well as a couple of shoppers, and of course we print fliers, advertising inserts, that sort of thing. It's the printing that pays the bills.''

"Then why do you call it Brave Wolf Publishing?''

Hunter scanned the red-rimmed hills. "Because printing is only the bread and butter of the business. the *Plaintalker* is its heart and soul.''

"It must have taken some doing to drum up that much business around here.''

"You bet it did. We needed off-reservation advertisers and printing jobs to make it go. A lot of people don't trust Indian businesses, and we had to prove ourselves—compete in quality and cost.''

"Your newspaper experience must've given you some extra credibility.''

"That and the fact that I was willing to put everything I had into this thing. We have to learn to help ourselves, Erin. It's the only way we're going to regain our self-respect.''

They'd reached the corner post of the wire fence that surrounded the cemetery. "Have you heard about Marlys's new project?'' Erin asked, complying with the unspoken mutual decision to stop there.

"Yes.''

"Do you think it will work?''

Hunter leaned against the fence post and let his eyes wander over the scattered array of small white crosses and narrow marble slabs. "It conflicts with some firmly established ways of doing things. Those are the kinds of problems people usually keep to themselves. I don't know.'' He shrugged. "Maybe Marlys can pull it off.''

"Maybe I can help her pull it off.'' When she heard the words out loud, she liked the sound of them.

"You?"

Erin nodded. "I've agreed to help get it started. They needed an inexpensive professional counselor. I'm a licensed social worker, you know."

"Licensed to practice on Indians?" The change in his tone came as a surprise, and Erin regarded him with a wordless question. "For how long, Erin?"

A slight frown crept over her forehead. "As long as it takes to get things started, I guess."

He snorted. "You're pretty good at getting things started and then taking your leave, aren't you?"

"I don't think you can say I was the one who got things started between us," Erin replied, her voice soft, controlled.

"Maybe not," he agreed, his control matching hers, "but you ended them." The look between them was hard until she glanced away. She heard him sigh. "Look, Erin, it's like I said. We have to learn to help ourselves. We get too many consultants who are here today and gone tomorrow. This should be Marlys's project."

"It is. The church fathers wanted credentials, and mine were handy. I'm not even sure I know how to go about starting something like this, but I'm here, and I'm going to give it a shot."

"What about your sister?"

"I haven't forgotten about her. Louise's murderer won't go unpunished if I can help it."

Hunter shook his head as he handed her the reins to the saddled horse and took Gambler for himself. "Games, Erin. You play too many games."

She watched him lever himself easily onto the horse's back. "I'm not playing games."

His silhouette loomed above her, outlined against the fading pink sky. "We don't have much of a rule book out here, you know. We're a culture without a written language, so everything's handed down by word of mouth. That way the rules can change with the times. Pretty hard for someone like you to play with us, though. You like to have it all down in black and white."

"I don't know what you're talking about," Erin protested, settling herself into the saddle.

"I'm talking about games, Erin." Hunter coaxed Gambler to walk ahead. "There've been some rule changes since we last played."

In the near darkness, with his back to her, Erin felt Hunter's silent chuckle.

# Chapter 3

"I have a job for you."

Erin glanced up from her ledger, wondering how Marlys always managed to look so comfortable in a dress. The July heat had kept Erin in shorts and tank tops, and she'd taken to clipping her hair up off her neck with a barrette. Marlys's triumphant smile exposed a slightly irregular row of very white teeth as she plunked a manila envelope on top of Erin's ledger.

"I haven't finished the last one you gave me," Erin said. "I'm just getting the hang of it. Bookkeeping isn't exactly my field, you know."

"Looks good to me." Marlys skimmed a forefinger down the page as she claimed the chair in front of Erin's work table. "Nice even columns."

"Well, it's my own system. I hope the board doesn't decide to audit us."

"I won't worry about it unless they do."

Erin pushed the ledger away, dropping her pencil into the center of the book. "Marlys, your bookkeeper-inventory supervisor-loom mender and coffee maker is really a social worker with no clients. Are you sure I'm really needed here?"

"It's only been three weeks since we opened the center, and the crafting is going great guns. The rest will come once the women see this as *their* place to come. And you're doing just what you need to do to make them feel comfortable around you."

"But you've billed this as strictly a craft center, not as a safe house. There's been no mention of—"

"Oh, yes there has. We're getting the word out in our own way, Erin. You can't go around putting up posters about a thing like this. Word of mouth works best around here."

"So I've been told." The manila envelope beckoned. Erin reached in and pulled out some papers. "What's this?"

"A printing order. We need some fliers." Marlys cocked her head and grinned.

"And you want me to take it to McLaughlin." A nod confirmed Erin's guess, but her own easy nod of agreement came as something of a surprise to Marlys. "I want to find out about getting a catalog printed, too," Erin said. "And the lines on these pages are beginning to converge right before my very eyes."

Bernadette Barker greeted all customers at Brave Wolf Publishing with a dazzling smile. She was her boss's ace in the hole, and she knew it. Any customer who didn't appreciate Hunter's strictly business approach could probably be won over by Bernadette's warmth. A man got the impression that Bernadette had been waiting all day just to talk to him and that every detail of his business was of major concern to her. Even women generally responded to Bernadette's friendly manner, but when she turned her charm on Erin O'Neill, she knew immediately that it wasn't working. And when Hunter emerged from his office and she saw the look in Erin's eyes, she knew why.

"Miss O'Neill has an order for us, and she doesn't seem to think I can handle it," Bernadette announced as Hunter approached the reception counter. "Do you have a few minutes?"

Hunter gave his co-worker a teasing smile. He was dressed casually in a short-sleeved yellow Western shirt and neatly cut tan pants. "You mean you can't convince Miss O'Neill that you know as much about this business as I do, Bernie?" He transferred the smile Erin's way. "She does, you know."

"I'm sure she does." Erin glanced from one to the other and wondered why seeing them standing behind the counter together made her uncomfortable. "This is an order for the church. I thought you might want to..."

"Ah, the lady is looking for a special deal," Hunter assumed, offering Bernadette a consoling pat on a shoulder left bare by her white sundress. "That *is* my department. Come on in my office, Erin."

Following Hunter's lead, Erin dropped a smile over her shoulder. "Thank you, Bernie."

Hunter's office was too small for the number of metal file cabinets and shelves full of boxes and books that were in it. Still, it was orderly in its crowded way, and there was room for a desk under the room's single window and a couple of chairs. Hunter offered Erin one of them before he took the one behind the desk. The back support creaked as he leaned against it, propping one foot on an open desk drawer. "What can I do for you, Erin?"

She handed him the envelope. "This is an order for fliers."

"The church gets a twenty percent discount. And Bernie does take care of this sort of thing." He set the envelope aside and gave her an expectant look.

"We want to have a catalog printed, and I thought you might give us some ideas."

"What kind of a catalog?"

"Something splashy with pictures of the items we'll have available for sale."

"We don't do four-color printing here, but I can get it done for you."

"Can you give me an idea of what we'd need?"

"In the way of money?" He shook his head. "Not until you tell me what you want—how many pages, what kind of paper you want. Then we can get bids." Lowering his foot, he leaned forward, resting his forearms on the desk. He looked at her with some interest now. "If you do your own layouts, you'll save money. The closer you can come to a camera-ready layout, the more you'll save."

"I'll need to find a photographer," Erin said, considering.

"I can do the photography myself. And I can help you with layouts." Erin's surprise was apparent. "The craft center is a good idea," he told her. "With the right kind of exposure it could really fly."

"But you have your doubts about the rest of the project."

His gesture was noncommittal. "Have you plied your real trade over there yet?"

Erin glanced down at the desk top and found herself concentrating on his hands as he absently fingered his pencil. "The refuge really hasn't been...active yet," she admitted. "My services in that department haven't been needed."

He should have felt some satisfaction in the answer. After all, he'd been more than skeptical. But he couldn't help thinking that if her services weren't needed, she'd leave. She'll leave anyway, sooner or later, he told himself, but some part of him answered that even much later would be too soon. "We all know the need is there," he heard himself assure her.

"But you don't think I'm the one to deal with that need," she said, meeting his challenge with bold green eyes.

"What I think won't change anything. The need is there. You'll get your opportunity in time to find out whether you're the one who can deal with it. Meanwhile, we'll get your catalog printed." He pushed his chair back and rose to his feet. "Would you like to see the rest of the plant?" he asked.

Erin had one more request, but she decided to wait with that. Perhaps giving her a tour would leave him more disposed to grant it. "Yes," she said with a smile. "I'd like that very much."

Hunter took her through a large room where several desks were buried under layout sheets, printed blocks of advertising and pictures. Various tools of the layout artist's trade were in evidence. There were also typewriters and three computers in the room. A heavyset young Indian woman was busy at the compositor, setting type. The oversize metal door to another room flew open, and a small, wiry, bronze-skinned man popped in. He wore grubby jeans and a coating of ink on his fingers.

"You rollin', Ross?" Hunter asked.

"I'm rollin', boss." The two grinned with pleasure at what was obviously a standing office quip.

"Right this way," Hunter invited, his hand at the back of Erin's waist. "The press is about to roll."

The press was housed in an adjoining room that seemed like a huge garage. By any city newspaper's standards it wouldn't have been impressive, but Hunter's pride shone in his dark eyes. "It's called a web press," he explained, and he drew lines in the air in front of them to call attention to the web of paper strung among the big rollers. Erin imagined a huge spider weaving strips of newsprint from one drum to the next. A buzzer warned that the press was about to roll, and Ross settled a headsetlike device over his ears just as the machine spun into motion.

The roar of the press startled Erin, and she backed against Hunter's chest. The hand he settled over her shoulder felt warm and natural, and she lost touch with the explanation he was shouting into her ear as his other hand drew more pictures in the air. When the noise stopped Erin waited for Hunter to move away first. Hunter waited, too. "Wanna see the darkroom?"

Erin slid a glance over her shoulder and caught the twinkle in his eye.

"It's my favorite part of the building," Hunter said, indicating the big door with a jerk of his chin. "Back this way."

They ran into Bernadette on their way back through the workroom, and she danced out of the way with a cheery, "How's the tour going?"

"It's fascinating," Erin reported.

"Be sure he shows you the darkroom. That's my favorite part of this business," Bernadette said, seating herself at a desk.

"That makes two of you," Erin mumbled, hurrying to catch the door Hunter held open for her.

"I've got one good photographer besides myself," Hunter explained, "but Bernie has taken an interest in it lately, and she's coming along nicely." Another door took them into the photography lab. "I don't know what I'd do without that woman. She had no previous training, but she's taken to the newspaper business like a duck to water."

"Really." Hadn't he noticed that her hair color wasn't natural?

"Here's where we make the negatives for the aluminum plates you saw on the press drums."

A huge camera was built into a wall between two small rooms. Hunter explained that the camera-ready page was set up in front of the camera on one side of the wall. "The photographer shoots the negative from this side," he continued, taking her hand and drawing her into the dark room. He shut the door, and they were bathed in red light. "Eerie, isn't it? Ever been in a darkroom?"

Erin surveyed the array of square pans, the bottles and boxes, the strips of negatives clipped to a line of string. The chemical smell was familiar. "Of course. I had a boyfriend who was the photographer for the school yearbook."

"Really." Probably the type who came up with stuff like, "Let's go in the darkroom and see what develops," Hunter thought.

Erin felt him standing close at her back, and the room grew warm. "You're a photographer as well as a reporter?" she asked, making some attempt to make sense of a negative that dangled in front of her nose. His hand touched her shoulder, and she drew a shallow breath.

"I was a reporter with the *Times*," he said quietly in her ear. "I learned enough about photography to get by." He turned her toward him and found that she was nibbling at her lower lip. Ducking a hanging lamp, he freed her lip with his thumb and cupped his hand under her jaw. Her features were so delicate, so irresistibly fine, that they deserved to be nibbled only by someone who would take great care not to bruise them, he thought. Someone like himself.

"Bernie will be wondering..."

"Let her wonder," he whispered, covering her mouth with the soft, light touch of his. Erin tipped her head back and touched his shirtfront with her fingertips. Yes, let her, she thought. She let his tongue hover over the ledge of her lower lip before she dropped it just enough to be an invitation. He accepted, and his tongue delved deeper for a taste that only left him wanting more.

"This isn't wise," she managed when his lips left hers.

He lifted his head and bumped it on the lamp. "It just isn't practical...at the moment." Turning her toward the door, he added, "And it's too damned hot in here."

"I thought this was your favorite part of the building—yours and Bernie's," she reminded him.

He opened the door and took a deep breath of cooler air. "Yeah, well...I never noticed how hot it was before."

After returning her to his office, Hunter tapped the manila envelope on his desk with outstretched finger. "This will be ready tomorrow," he promised, facing her as he balanced himself against the front edge of the desk. "Unless you want to wait."

"I'm in no hurry," she replied. "While I'm waiting, I wonder if you'd mind if I went through the back issues of your paper?"

"Back, say about six months?"

She felt awkward standing at attention with her request while he sat casually on the edge of his desk letting his eyes tell her how foolish he thought she was being. But she persisted. "Back even further, I think. I'd like to read about the camp before...before the murder took place there...as well as..."

"I'm sure you kept up with all that in the national media." He folded his arms over his chest. She was being tested.

"I want to read what you had to say. I want to know what *you* think it's all about."

"Why?"

"Because I respect your opinion," she said honestly. "And I want to understand."

She knew the raised brow and the slight nod of his head were his indication that he accepted her explanation. He waved his hand at an array of large cardboard file boxes on a shelf. "Help yourself. You can have the office."

"Oh, no, I don't mean to..."

"I don't need it." He reached for a handful of papers, took up the envelope that held her order and then left the desk for her use. "I have other things I need to do. The rest of the staff will be knocking off pretty soon, but take your time. I plan to work late."

"Thank you."

For the next several hours Erin was immersed in the *Plaintalker*. She had no sense of the passage of time, took no notice of when activity in the building shut down, lost touch with herself entirely. At some point Hunter appeared with a can of Orange Crush, and she thanked him as he left, flicking on a light switch on his way out. Popping open the can, she allowed herself a moment in the present. Only Hunter would remember her penchant for Orange Crush. She smiled to herself and returned to her reading.

She had followed the Crimson Eagle Camp story in the national media, but the stories in the pages of the *Plaintalker* offered a new perspective. Hunter talked about the issue from many sides. He featured the idealistic activists, who wanted desperately to grab the world by its ears and make it look at the reservation as a fact of American life. He editorialized about the activists without ideals—those who used the publicity and the contributions and the heat of the moment for their own ends. A story about an unemployed Indian construction worker living in Rapid City revealed the frustration of a man who believed that the activity at Crimson Eagle led employers to mistrust Indians in general. There was an interview with an old man whose words rang hollow with hopelessness. The red man's lot was the same as it had been since he was a boy, and he didn't see that "a bunch of young folks making a fuss on a hill" would change anything.

Hunter hadn't gotten much out of anyone who worked for the Department of the Interior, but the governor had derided the movement, calling it the brainchild of "a bunch of hippies." In an editorial Hunter noted that the governor's epithet was dated at best, and that it betrayed his lack of understanding of the people who lived in the forgotten pockets in his state.

Erin read Hunter's anger and frustration in the writing that dealt with Louise's death. He called her a friend and despaired the senseless loss of her life. In several of his editorials, though, he referred to the influence of outsiders, whose motivations he apparently considered suspect. Louise was a friend, but she'd had no business there, Erin surmised, and he obviously included Erin in that judgment, too.

Twelve years ago he'd asked her to stay. When she'd insisted on returning home to finish school, he'd asked her to come back, and she hadn't hesitated to give him her promise. Of course she would come back. She loved him. She belonged there with him. Neither of them had questioned that fact on the day she kissed him goodbye and boarded an eastbound plane.

But that had been a different Hunter—a younger Hunter, who'd lived and loved in the present moment with such a fierce, intense flame that Erin had wondered where he'd find fuel for tomorrow's fire. Here, in these pages, she realized that he had his own source of fire, and the flame within him burned hot and steady. He believed in what he was doing, and that was the source of his energy. He had no patience with those who stopped to warm themselves only in passing at someone else's fire.

His thoughts on tribal politics fascinated her. The man who had once seemed content with the living he could make riding herd on someone else's cows and making an eight-second ride on a bucking horse now contemplated the lack of possibilities for employment on isolated reservation land, which had been left to the Indians mainly because its agricultural prospects were so bleak. Some of his editorials criticized the stubborn prejudices of the non-Indians, and others criticized the prejudices of his own people. He pointed to the stagnation of the Bureau of Indian Affairs and the need for a degree of independence from that caretaker agency. And he pointed to the need for reform within the tribal government. Comments on the last probably took the greatest courage of all to make.

A white paper bag plopped on the desk in front of her, and Erin started up from her chair with a gasp.

"If you're going to read through the night, you'd better sustain yourself with some food." Hunter grinned, enjoying the innocent look of surprise in the clear, round pools of her green eyes. With her blond hair pulled up off her neck and the straight, spiky bangs framing her oval face, she looked just as he enjoyed remembering her, innocently surprised and then, with the sparkling smile that echoed in those green re-

flecting pools, childishly delighted when he did some
little thing to please her.

"What time is it? I got so interested in these, I guess
I lost track." She glanced down at the bag. "I'm not
keeping you from something, am I?"

"Just supper, which, such as it is, I lay before you."
A cardboard drink tray with two large, plastic-topped
paper cups was added to the offering. He dragged a
chair up to the desk and sank into the vinyl seat.

"Orange Crush?" she asked.

"Naturally."

Erin opened the bag and stuck her nose in the top.
"Pizza burgers and fries?" From the expectation in
her voice, she might have been clarifying the identity
of filet mignon.

"Only the very best," he assured her.

"Oh, heavenly!" she gasped at a whiff of what was
inside. One well-manicured hand dived into the bag.
"How often I've craved just this combination. I've
tried to recapture it, but the sauce was never quite
right, or they didn't have Crush." She glanced up
anxiously. "Did you get plenty of ketchup?"

Laughing, he produced a red plastic squeeze bottle
from behind his chair. "Plenty of ketchup."

"You stole that!"

"I'll take it back tomorrow."

She shook her head, laughing with him. "In some
ways you haven't changed at all."

"In some ways." A pregnant silence followed, and
then he held out an open palm. "Are you going to
share?"

Erin spread the feast on Hunter's desk, and they dug in with relish, each devouring two pizza burgers and lavishing ketchup on the mound of crisp fries.

"Well, you were in here long enough to read everything on those shelves." Hunter made a pointed survey of the stack of papers on the desk and the file boxes lined up on the floor. "Find anything interesting?"

"Mmm." Swallowing a mouthful of pizza burger, she hastened to assure him, "Don't worry. I'll put it all back exactly the way it was. And, yes, it was all interesting—every word. You're a very good writer, Hunter."

"I don't put out the *Plaintalker* single-handedly," he reminded her, pleased with her reaction to the paper.

"Of course not, but your style is distinctive. After reading all this, I think I could write a dissertation on it. I had no idea—" She cut herself off, and he gave her a knowing look.

"You had no idea I could write? Brace yourself, Erin. I can read and cipher, too."

Her sigh wasn't an apology, but a recognition of what she'd missed seeing in him. "Your interests seemed to center around wild horses and country music. We used to talk about things like pizza burgers and drive-in movies."

"And the color of the sunset, and how long it would take us to walk to the moon." Pleased with the memory, he settled back in his chair and watched her lower her lashes over her pink blush.

"Why didn't you speak of these other things back then?" she asked as she trailed the end of a French fry along the edge of the paper basket.

"I can't say they were important to me then." He studied her. Would it have made a difference? he wondered.

"Some of those editorials must have had your phone ringing off the hook," she suggested quickly, changing the tone. "I can't believe you accused the tribal chairman's closest adviser of going on a junket. How did you get away with that?"

Hunter smiled, remembering the man's angry tirade right there in his office. "I was told to be off the reservation before the sun rose on another day."

"And?"

"And when the sun came up I was still here. I never heard another word about it."

"Do you get a lot of threats?" she wondered.

"A few," he admitted, reaching for his drink. "All pretty much the same caliber." A long pull drained the contents of the paper cup, and he tossed it in the wastebasket with a thunk. "Empty. But you can't please all the people all the time. Not in this business."

"Your comments on the BIA get pretty scathing."

"They've all been made before," Hunter acknowledged with a shrug. "The bureau is intent on perpetuating itself. It's made us dependents of the federal government. 'Wards,' they call us. But any talk of eliminating it becomes frightening. What would happen to the treaties? What about medical care, education, basic subsistence? What about our rights? We're up to our chins in a bureaucratic quagmire, and we're afraid if we fish around our ankles for our bootstraps, we'll drown."

Leaning intently into the conversation, Erin asked, "So what's the answer?"

"Luckily, I don't have to have answers." His one-sided smile was almost self-deprecating. "My job doesn't require them. I just keep hammering away at the questions."

"And doing a good job of it." Erin began stuffing the sandwich wrappings back into the paper bag as she added, "Most people want to skip the questions and go straight to the answers."

He leaned forward to help her clear the desk. "The answers change from person to person, from week to month to year. The questions are the only constant."

They reached for the ketchup bottle at the same time, and his hand closed over hers. "I've asked myself the same question over and over again for twelve years, Erin."

The quiet resolution in his voice made her shiver. "Answers change because people change," she said. Her voice sounded thin and distant in her own ears, and she knew he must feel her pulse racing. She met his gaze. "And timeless questions find new answers."

The question that burned in his eyes was one he'd only begun to ask himself since she'd come back. How much have you changed, Erin? How much?

A distant, explosive crack rent the moment. Erin could only compare the sound to the backfire of a car, but she felt Hunter stiffen, his neck craning like an animal scenting the air. With another crack, the window just above Erin's shoulder shattered.

"Erin, get down!"

With a gasp, Erin braced her hands against the desk, poised to bolt. Before she could move Hunter flattened her over the desk and covered her with his body. Another shot rang out. "My God!" Hunter breathed. "Erin? You okay?"

## Chapter 4

Erin couldn't answer. Sandwiched between the desk top and Hunter's heavy torso, she could hardly breathe. Closest to her face was her own outstretched hand, and beyond that the desk was strewn with shattered glass.

Hunter moved quickly to Erin's side of the desk, kicking the desk lamp's plug out of the wall as he went. He kept her down with protective forearms and pulled her with him to the floor as soon as he reached her.

Industrial-grade carpet chafed her cheek. "Hunter, what's going on?" she managed under the pressure of his weight.

"I don't know. I have to shut off the overhead light. You stay down." He eased away from her, and her head bobbed up as she lifted her chest to fill it with air.

Her cheek was flattened against the carpet again. "I said stay down," he growled. "Flat."

Erin tucked her chin and squirmed against the floor, rotating her position until she could see Hunter, who was doing a low-profile scramble toward the far wall. He reached up and threw the room into darkness. The action was answered by another distant crack and more shattering glass. "I hope you're insured," Erin muttered.

"Me too." He thought better of making any comment about the kind of insurance they might be needing.

She heard him moving about and wished he'd come back to her. A metal locker door was opened, and he shuffled some things around before finding what he wanted. Dark forms were beginning to take shape before Erin's eyes, and one of them slid along the floor in her direction. He swore under his breath, an expletive she remembered as an old favorite of his.

"Is someone shooting at us?" she asked finally.

"Looks that way."

"At *us*?"

"So far he's only hit windows. I'm hoping that's all he's shooting at." Reaching over the desk, he grabbed the phone. "Damn it," he said after a moment. "He's thorough."

"You can't . . . call for help?"

"Line's dead." Biting out an expression of frustration, he slid down beside her, and they heard another glass-shattering shot elsewhere in the building. Erin scooted in close to Hunter's side. "You okay?" he asked.

"I'm fine. If he keeps shooting like that, someone will hear it."

"Maybe." He settled an arm around her, as much to reassure himself as to comfort her. "We're sitting pretty far out on the edge of town. What did you think the sound was when you first heard it?"

"I didn't know. A car backfiring or something. I've never been around guns."

"You came out here to play detective, and you've never been around guns? Fine thinking, Erin O'Neill. You and most of the rest of the town would be startled by the noise, shrug it off as some kid with a few leftover firecrackers, and go back to your business. If we're lucky, maybe some cop'll hear it."

"And if we're not?"

Hunter sighed. Their situation was about as unlucky as he cared to consider. "Erin, I don't know what's going on here. I don't know who's out there, and I don't know whether he wants me dead or just shaking in my boots."

"Are you...shaking in your boots?" she asked hesitantly.

*Hell, yes.* "Hell, no. Steady as a rock." He hugged her a little tighter and pushed back a fleeting mental picture of Louise. "Brave's my middle name."

"You'll be able to get us out of this, then, right? What are we going to do?"

"We're going to hide."

"Oh." Her voice fell.

"I think we'll be safest in the darkroom. Part of a hunter's expertise is in knowing when to stalk and when to hide."

"And your first name is Hunter," she acknowledged. He pulled his arm away and rolled to his side. Erin heard several metallic clicks. "What are you doing?"

"It's so damned dark in here, I'm not sure," he grumbled. "I think I'm loading a pistol."

"I thought we were just going to hide. What are you going to do with a gun?" She pictured him sneaking out the back door with a gun in his hand and getting shot the minute he stepped outside.

"I'm just going to keep it handy. He's got one. I figure I oughta have one, too. You ready?"

Without waiting for an answer Hunter sprang into a crouched run, pulling Erin behind him with the order that she "keep down." She imagined them playing cowboys and Indians with one of the neighborhood kids. If only somebody would call the other kid home for supper now, he'd have to yell, "Ally ally out's in free!" A nervous giggle bubbled in Erin's throat.

"You've got a strange sense of humor, lady," Hunter grumbled, squeezing her hand as he quickened his pace.

"This isn't real, Hunter. It's funny because it isn't real." As she rounded a corner unexpectedly her shoulder slammed into a doorframe, and she grabbed Hunter's forearm for support. He stiffened, his breath hissing between his teeth, and her hand came away wet and sticky. "What's this?" she gasped.

"Real blood," he told her. "Mine."

"Oh, Hunter, no! Is it bad?"

"It's just a cut. I ran into some glass on the floor. Bernie stashes first-aid kits all over the place." They'd reached the darkroom, and Hunter was fumbling for the doorknob. "Hope she's got one in here."

Erin followed the tug of her hand. They were in the heart of the building, and it was pitch dark. Another window shattered as Hunter flicked a switch and bathed them in red light. "He's still with us."

"Why will we be safer in here?" Erin asked Hunter's back as he searched the top shelf of another metal locker.

"No windows, no glass. This room's hard to find in the dark." Their assailant had a high-powered rifle. A bullet could penetrate the outside wall, but Erin didn't need to know that.

"But what if he does find it?"

Hunter elbowed the locker door shut as he turned, a box in one hand, the pistol, pointing at the floor, in the other. "If he comes through the door I'll plug him. But it won't come to that. I think he's playing games with us."

"Cowboys and Indians?" Erin asked, reaching for Hunter's arm, which dripped dark red. "Doesn't he know the rules? Everybody quits when it gets dark."

"What did I tell you about the rules out here, Erin? If you can get away with it, it's legal." He allowed himself to be taken to the sink, thinking that he'd enjoy having her fuss over a little cut on his arm. He handed her the first-aid kit.

"He won't get away with this," Erin insisted, discovering the gauze pads and antiseptic. "We'll find out who's out there, and we'll see that he's arrested and charged."

"We will?"

"Of course. People simply cannot go around shooting at people."

Hunter inclined his head in the shooter's direction. "Somebody ought to tell him that. He probably hasn't heard."

"Oh, Hunter, these crimes can't go unpunished. People around here have to start demanding justice. Where are the police? Look at Louise...."

"Yes. Look at Louise." Suddenly impatient with Erin's dainty dabbing at him, Hunter shoved his arm under the running water, washed the blood away and shut the faucet off. He took a pad of gauze from the box and pressed it tightly against the cut. "You can demand justice all you want, Erin, but the fact is that people *can* go around shooting at people, and people who get shot at sometimes get killed. *You* won't be finding out who's out there. You'll be reporting it to the police as soon as we get out of here. And I'll be reporting it to the public."

"I know how those things go," Erin mumbled, waving his hand aside so she could reapply the antiseptic he'd washed off. He let her dab at him again before he replaced the bloody gauze pad with a fresh one.

"You know how those things go, do you? You think a three-month stint twelve years ago made you an expert on reservation life?" He watched her wrap his arm with a strip of gauze bandage. "Tighter," he instructed. "I'll see to getting any revenge we might need. It's probably a safe bet I'm the one he's shooting at."

Erin's back stiffened; she was senselessly indignant at being excluded as a target. They were together in this. "How do you know it's a *he*? Maybe it's your girl Friday, and maybe she's shooting at *me*."

"Bernie?" He glanced up, surprised by the suggestion. The hint of coyness in her eyes made him grin. "Why would Bernie want to shoot at you?"

"Because it looks like I'm about to spend the night with her boss in her favorite part of the building."

"It does, doesn't it?" He chuckled as he examined the bandage.

Erin sobered. "He'll give up at daylight, won't he?"

"I would, if I were him."

"Then we're probably stuck until then, right?"

"I'd say so," Hunter judged. "Unless somebody misses you before then. Any chance Marlys might be looking for you?"

"Marlys sent me over here. She knows I'm with you."

"And if you don't come back at a reasonable hour..."

"Marlys will mind her own business. I don't have a curfew anymore."

Hunter smiled at the reference to a time when staying out late was delightfully chancy. "We came up with some dandy excuses for missing curfew, but this one would've topped them all."

Erin looked down at the bandage on his arm. The red light camouflaged her blush as she recalled all she'd dared to do just to be with him. Only on the final dare had she proved herself a coward.

She was such a lady, he thought, watching her drop her eyes at what he knew was in her mind. It was in his, as well. She had always been a lady, even when he'd taken her to the most isolated stand of cottonwoods he could find and coaxed her to make love with him there in the prickly scrub grass. She'd struggled with the right and wrong of it, with the impropriety and inconvenience of it, but he'd always known that the love would come. She'd look up at him, and it would come, warm and sweet in those trusting green eyes. Once she'd given him that look he could think of nothing else but making her his.

"You did a good job, Erin," he said quietly. "Thanks."

"What?" She glanced up and then down again. "Oh. Do you think it's stopped bleeding?"

He nodded. "I'd say 'Make yourself comfortable,' but I'm afraid that's going to be an impossibility. The linoleum's going to get pretty hard." Then he remembered something and stepped just outside the door to retrieve a folded tarp, which he dropped on the floor next to the wall. "Painter's tarp. Have a seat."

"You're the boss, baby," Erin quipped as she knelt on the tarp.

The significance of the coffee mug quotation dawned on him, and a slow grin spread across his face as he joined her, settling his back against the wall. "You know something, Erin O'Neill? If you hadn't ditched me for greener pastures quite some time ago, I'd start thinking you might be jealous."

"Jealous of Blondie? Hardly. She bleaches her hair."

Typical female observation, he thought with a satisfied smile. "Blondie's my dog," he pointed out. "Bernie's my... my right-hand man."

"Nicely put, Hunter. Very unsexist. I didn't 'ditch' you 'for greener pastures.'" She had hurled herself from one topic to the other without pause for second thoughts. It gave her the impetus to continue. "I gave it a great deal of thought. I plotted it out in my mind a hundred different ways, and ninety-nine of them didn't work. We were just . . . too different."

"What about the hundredth?" he asked, his voice sounding strangely hollow.

Erin sighed and dropped her head back against the wall. "The hundredth was the one I tucked away, the one I kept for myself for the times when I needed . . . a secret treasure."

"One out of a hundred," he said. "Pretty risky odds." The neutrality in his tone sounded so convincing that he even had himself believing none of it bothered him anymore. "You went for security, then. Did you find better odds?"

Risky odds, better odds. Hunter and Arthur. She'd been offered love behind door number one and security behind door number two. It had been like one of those folktales in which you only learn the significance of your choice after you've made it. "Yes. If my life with Arthur was anything, it was secure."

"Wasn't he . . . good to you?" The question had been carefully phrased. Hunter really didn't want to know what Arthur Bates had been to Erin. But if he'd hurt her, if the man had been cruel to her in any way . . .

"He was courteous," she said. "He gave the full measure of his respect to my . . . position as his wife."

"And were you happy with your position?" he asked.

"I guess I was content with it for a while. I kept thinking there was more to come."

"Children?"

The word on Hunter's lips made her heart swell. When Arthur had said it, she'd shrunk back in horror. "We had sense enough to realize that the marriage wasn't a good one. Children wouldn't have made it any better."

Should he lie to her and say he was sorry she hadn't found happiness with another man? He wasn't sorry. He was relieved. He'd hoped he was a bigger man than that, but he guessed he wasn't. "Sounds as though you thought out the breakup as carefully as you planned the marriage," he observed.

Had she? Had Arthur's talent for planning rubbed off on her? She didn't remember it that way. She remembered the feeling of suffocation, and she remembered finally managing to gasp, "I want out." With those words a weight had been lifted from her chest, and she had breathed deeply for the first time in years. She knew then that the weight had been one of her own design.

"My planning hasn't always been the best, but I'm regrouping now. I'm trying a new approach," she concluded. "What about you? Have you really found what you want?"

"I've found something that needs doing, and I know I'm the one to do it. I had a good job out in L.A., but when I resigned there were twenty good reporters ready to take my place. Here there's only me."

"Don't forget Bernie." Oh, why did I say that?

He knew why, and he knew she wanted to bite her tongue for it. He gave her a sidelong glance and a half grin. "Bernie isn't easily forgotten. Our advertising accounts are proof of that. She keeps 'em coming back."

"Does she now?" Erin muttered.

Another distant crack sounded in the night, and more glass tinkled. Wide-eyed, Erin leaned closer to Hunter, and he took the opportunity to lift an arm over her head and lay it across her shoulders. "Maybe he's just a vandal," Erin suggested, as though the label made the assailant somehow less threatening. "Maybe he doesn't think anyone's here."

"He saw the light go out," he reminded her, stroking her shoulder in a soothing gesture.

"Why doesn't he come after us, then? Why is he just sitting out there taking pot shots at the building? It's nerve-racking."

"I think that's the whole point."

She thought about it for a moment and decided it was an effective strategy. "I'm scared."

He pulled her closer so she would rest her head against him. He called on his wellspring of self-control as he told himself to hold her, just hold her. "I was, too, at first," he confessed. "But now I think he's going to stay where he is, which means we're all right where we are. By morning he'll be gone, like a bad dream."

She didn't believe the part about his being scared. "I thought you never got scared, Brave Wolf. You used to challenge the gods at every opportunity." She heard the chuckle deep in his throat and felt the steady cadence of his heartbeat in his chest. Her body relaxed into a comfortable awareness of his physical strength. "What about your middle name?"

"I've learned its true meaning. There was a time when I was too foolish to be scared, or too proud to admit it." *I never told you how much you scared me—*

how I was afraid of loving you. "Fear comes first," he told her. "Then it's possible to be brave."

"They've done this to you before, haven't they?" she guessed.

"Somebody shot out the windows in the van once."

"Did you ever find out who or why?"

"Never found out who for sure, though some names were tossed around. There was a feud going on between the Indian landowners and the Indian cattlemen over lease rates. I covered the landowners' side one week, and that's when the windows went." He shifted gears with a noncommittal shrug. "The next week I covered the cattlemen's side, and someone slashed the tires."

"Sounds like a no-win situation."

"Yeah, but when I did an editorial the third week suggesting some common ground, some possible compromises, I got good responses from both sides. So there's hope."

"Who have you offended lately?" Erin wondered.

"My insurance man. I'm becoming a high risk." He suspected that this involved the activists at Crimson Eagle, and it might tempt Erin's pretty little nose. Best he avoid it with her, he thought. His embrace tightened just slightly.

"You always were," she muttered.

"And what about you, Erin? Don't you think you're a risk?"

"Me?" She tilted her head back with the question and caught his hooded stare. Swallowing, she managed a raspy, "Why?"

"Look at you. The years have taken nothing away from you. If anything, you're more beautiful than I remembered."

She watched his jaw become rigid and knew there were words he was biting back. She wanted to hear them. Whatever they were, the demand for them coursed recklessly through her body. "How does that put you at risk, Hunter?"

He took one deep breath, the muscles in his jaw working against an answer. But she was too close. Her lips, parted slightly on the echo of his name, were too moist and inviting, and suddenly he was too hungry. He bent his head and seized the kiss she offered. Her mouth was hotter than he'd expected. His kiss was as demanding as she remembered. The fusion was instantaneous. With a groan Hunter moved his hand to cup her breast.

His lips moved over her face, rediscovering the softness of her skin, the delicacy of her bone structure. Aristocratic, he thought. A face to be touched softly, and softly he touched her. His hand found its way under the summer top, freed the catch on her bra and greeted her breast with fingers that trembled as they sought her.

She arched into his hand. With his next kiss he lowered her back to the floor. She drank passion from his mouth, and the fire she'd banked twelve years before spread within her, licking the dormant places in her body with life-giving heat. He made her breasts tighten against his teasing lips, first nipping, then caressing her to an aching hardness that matched his own. She felt it against her thigh, and she shifted, inviting him to press the part of him she had aroused against the part of her that could best ease his tension. By turns they taunted one another and reveled in the sweet, sweet torment. She whispered his name. She groaned his name. This feeling was Hunter, and she'd known it only as Hunter. No other. Never any other.

"How much do you want to risk, Erin?" he growled, his hand poised at the clasp of her slacks. "Tell me what you want. Tell me what risks you'll take to have it."

Her reply was a desperate moan, a helpless sound that both drew him to her and frustrated him. He wanted an answer.

A sudden clatter somewhere in the building brought Hunter bolt upright. Confused, Erin followed his lead more slowly, but her chest heaved with her erratic breathing, just as his did. He listened. She breathed only a "Wh—" before his hand was over her mouth. They heard the sound again.

Hunter's instincts told him to wait, to let the predator become the prey, let him walk into the trap. But to let him come to Hunter was to let him come to Erin, and Hunter could not allow that. With his mouth against her ear, he breathed, "Don't move. Don't make a sound." He saw the terror in her eyes as she realized he was going to leave her. He caught the hand that reached for him and touched her fingertips to his lips. Taking the pistol, he shut off the red light and left the darkroom on silent feet.

Erin waited, pulling her clothing together as she strained her ears for sound. There was none. After what seemed like hours the door opened, and Erin froze. The light came on again.

"I forgot about Merlin," Hunter announced, producing a hank of black fur from behind his back.

"M-Merlin?"

"The resident cat. Bernie brought him in after a mouse ran across her feet."

"Oh," Erin sighed. "Bless Bernie's heart; she takes care of everything."

"I don't know what—"

"You'd do without her. Yes, I know."

Hunter lowered Merlin to the floor. Without so much as an investigation of the darkroom Merlin slunk back out the door, showing no patience with the interruption in his night's work. Erin's eyes followed the cat and watched the doorway long after he was out of sight. With a deep breath she looked back at Hunter. They'd come too close to complicating things. He'd touched her, and she'd forgotten where she was and what was going on around her. She hadn't even heard the sound that alerted him.

"Do you think he's still out there?" she asked finally.

"I don't think I want to go out and see."

"No, of course not," she agreed quickly. "We have to wait for daylight."

He closed the door, then dropped beside her on the tarp, laying the pistol aside and propping his back against the wall. "One of us should get some sleep," he suggested. "And since I'm the only one who knows something about guns it can't be me."

"I'll keep you company," she offered in a small voice. She felt a sudden shyness with him.

He raised a brow. "I think you'd be less of a temptation if you were asleep."

"Hunter, I—"

With a shake of his head, he cut her off. "I won't apologize if you'll do me the same courtesy. We may be as different as you say, but there's a chemistry between us. There always was."

"Yes. A . . . chemistry," she echoed.

"But at a hundred to one, I don't like the odds any better than you do. If it's just chemistry, we'd better stay out of the lab."

Erin looked around her. The bottles and boxes and eerie light reminded her of just that. "Your suggestion comes a little late."

In the red light his derisive smile took on a strange cast. "Do you want to experiment? I'm willing. Just remember what I said: the rules have changed." She glanced away. "No? Smart girl," he said, stretching his legs out in front of him. "Put your head in my lap and go to sleep, Erin. No risk involved. My promise."

Because she was tired, and because he seemed to want it that way, Erin complied. Hunter felt almost relieved when he knew she slept. He'd bet against the odds once before, and he'd lost. He knew now that Erin wasn't a gambler.

It was just past five when he shook her gently and spoke her name. It would be sunrise, and the town would be stretching its morning legs soon. He'd have to make a dash for the house and hope the telephone line was still intact there. Watching Erin turn over and flex her shoulders was pleasant enough. He smiled down at her. He was sure she wasn't aware of the endurance test she put him through when she rolled her head in his lap that way.

She squinted and groaned. "I've been dreaming in red. Am I awake now?"

"What do you see?"

"A red man."

"And what do you feel?"

"Ouch!" She jumped away from the pinch on her thigh, jackknifing upright.

"Right on both counts. You're awake, which is more than I can say for my leg." A quick massage revived his circulation before he peeled himself off the floor, stretching the stiffness out of one muscle at a time. "Hell of a way to spend a night. Next time you decide to sleep with me, Erin O'Neill, let's find ourselves a bed."

Erin's arms made wings at her sides as she used both hands to iron the kinks out of her spine. Eyes closed, she rolled her head until a dozen joints cracked. "Mmm. Next time I bring you a printing order, let's forgo the wild west show."

Hunter splashed cold water on his face, and Erin did the same. They turned to each other, dripping, and burst out laughing. "Now what?" Erin asked.

"I think I'll sprint over to the house and put the coffee on."

Her grin faded. "What about *him*?"

"Should we ask him to join us for coffee? He's put in a long night, too," Hunter suggested dryly.

"Very funny. Are you sure he's gone?"

"Almost sure," he said, retrieving the pistol from the floor. "I would be."

"Hunter, you're not a crazed gunman. You don't know how he thinks." She was following as he headed through another small room and down a hallway on his way to the front desk and the door. She kept up the protest. "Maybe we should wait until people start coming to work. We'd be sure he was gone if—"

"If he didn't shoot at anyone else. We've minimized the odds by waiting this long. Now it's time to move." At the door he turned to find her right behind him, apparently ready to follow. Did she really think he'd let her go out there yet? "It's time for *me* to move. You take this." He put the gun in her hand and curled her reluctant fingers around the handle.

"You might need it."

He shook his head. "It doesn't have that much range. It's only good for rattlesnakes and anyone you don't like who tries to come through this door."

She gave the weapon a distasteful look. "But I don't..."

"The hammer's sitting on an empty chamber." He smiled, his eyes sympathetic. "Just in case you have an itchy trigger finger. It'll just click the first time. The second time it'll go bang." He adjusted the pistol in her hand. "Hold it down and away from you."

"Hunter, please wait."

He gave her a quick kiss. "I'm just going to run over and plug in the coffeepot. I'll be right back. You stay put, no matter what. If the phone works I'll have the police here before you know it."

Erin stood back from a broken window and watched him launch his run to the house. *No matter what.* His long legs carried him in a crouching run over the newly mown prairie grass in a serpentine flight.

"Please, God," Erin whispered, holding the gun out from her body at the end of a stiff arm. When he reached the back door she allowed herself to breathe again.

"He sure left you a mess over there." Police Officer Joe Tiger closed the back door, and his boot heels scuffed across Hunter's kitchen floor. "Had any arguments with anyone this week, Hunter?"

"I've had a few with this lady, but she's got an airtight alibi." Hunter chuckled at his own joke until he caught the angry glance Erin's eyes threw his way. He shrugged. "Well, I do have to wonder why he shot out my windshield and not yours."

"Maybe he's a gentleman," Erin returned.

"We need a list of possibilities," the policeman said. "What have you been writing about, Hunter? Who've you offended lately?"

"Just the usual," Hunter said, lifting a noncommittal shoulder. "Rich men, poor men, beggar men, thieves."

"I hope you left the Indian chiefs alone," Erin put in. She didn't know how he could be so casual about this.

"What about those outlaws down at Crimson Eagle?" Tiger asked. "You've been making some pretty pointed suggestions about outside troublemakers, and there are a couple down there I've got my doubts about."

"Really?" Hunter sipped his coffee thoughtfully. With a chin jerk toward the counter, he offered, "Help yourself, Joe. What kind of doubts?"

Listening as she shared coffee with the two men, Erin had the feeling that there was more to be learned from what they left unsaid than from their conversation. Apparently most of the people at Crimson Eagle were known quantities, some better known than others. But there was one man who seemed to have come from nowhere, and who had gotten close to Johnny Parker since Johnny had assumed a leadership role.

After Joe Tiger left Erin asked Hunter about the so-called outside troublemaker. "Have you met him?"

"I've seen him," Hunter told her. "Whenever I'm around he just kind of fades back into the brush."

"Where do you think he's from?"

Hunter looked down into his black coffee, absently running his thumb over the curve of the mug's handle. "Johnny says New Mexico someplace."

"What do you say?"

He lifted his chin slowly and gave her a half-shuttered look. "I say Johnny knows him better than I do."

"Was he there when Louise was killed?"

He took a deep breath. "Don't meddle in it, Erin."

She leaned forward slightly, pressing. "But he's the one you meant when you wrote about outsiders who get involved in Indian politics, isn't he?"

"Among others," he admitted.

"What's his name?"

"I won't tell you that. You're an outsider, too."

"Maybe. But I buried a sister six months ago, and I just spent a whole night getting shot at myself. I think I've earned the right to a few answers," she informed him.

"As soon as I have any, I'll pass them on to you. *Answers*, not speculation. Meanwhile, I suggest you stick with your project at the mission. You're on safe ground there."

The discussion had reached a stalemate. When Erin left it was with a stomach full of tension and a head full of questions. How much of a threat did Hunter pose to this "outsider"? Enough to draw his fire the night before? Who was this man? What was his name? Had Louise known him? Hunter had criticized a lot of people, but Louise had never been critical. How did the two incidents fit together?

"Sam, this is Hunter. I need some information." Hunter hooked his boot heel over the bottom rung of the tall stool. Whenever he talked on the phone he doodled, and the pad on the counter in front of him already read "LAPD" in big block letters. He was working on "SAM."

"Sure, Hunter, if I can get it. What do you need?"

"I need a cop's nose and a red man's ears." Sam Whiteman had both. He'd been a detective with the Los Angeles Police since Hunter's early days as a reporter. With Sam as an ally Hunter had turned in some prizewinning stories.

"The Crimson Eagle thing? I think they've circled their wagons pretty tight up there."

"My office was shot up last night, Sam."

There was a pause at the other end, and then, with a new concern, came the question, "Where were you?"

"Sitting at my desk."

"I take it you ducked in time."

Hunter chuckled, remembering. "You'd have been proud of my reflexes, Sam."

"You cowboys are all reflex and no brain," Sam teased. "How can I help?"

"I'm interested in that bunch of terrorists you had some dealings with a while back—the ones who call themselves the Pan-Indian Liberators."

"You think you got one back there?"

"Maybe. Says he's from New Mexico, but it doesn't check out." Hunter's pencil had retraced "ERIN" several times before he caught himself. He tore the sheet off the pad and crumpled it in his palm.

"Got a photo?"

"Not yet," Hunter said, writing more block letters.

"Got a name?"

He studied the name on the pad. Probably an alias, but it was all he had. "Rick Morales."

# Chapter 5

The mission's center of activity was the dining hall. Upstairs there were offices, an infirmary, a large lounge, lately crowded with quilt frames, and a guest bedroom, which everyone called "the bishop's room." With the new craft center in full swing weekdays were the busiest. Having arranged their days to accommodate their crafting outside the home, many of the local women had informally become part of a morning, afternoon or evening group, with a few who stayed longer hours and some who visited infrequently just to see what was going on. Baby-sitters were hired to entertain the young children with outdoor activities, but many of the toddlers, contenting themselves with pacifiers of all kinds, stayed close to their mothers.

The chatter was low-key and incessant, some of it in Lakota, some in English, but much of it a combination of the two. Erin found the atmosphere relaxing, and though she knew she was still regarded as an outsider, her presence had become accepted. It was particularly enlightening to take a back seat and listen. In an area of very high unemployment, many of these women were the economic mainstays of their families in one way or another. They carried heavy loads. Yet the corners of their eyes crinkled readily with the laughter that punctuated so much of the conversation. Their eyes brightened continually in response to the dry humor they shared among themselves. Needles flew through colorful beads or pieces of fabric as the persistent teasing and easy laughter kept their own pace.

When she was finally included in the teasing Erin felt part of the group. She'd never been a crafter, but she didn't mind helping to keep the babies out of the sewing baskets and the coffee urn from going dry. Using her understanding of group dynamics, she was finding that these informal gatherings were as useful as the private counseling she had finally begun to do. Often, when the conversation turned serious, she was unobtrusively able to direct some real soul-searching. There were times when she found herself refereeing some heated disagreements, but more often the group enjoyed light banter, especially the deadpan put-ons that usually left Erin suspecting she'd been had.

"I really worked on this piece of hide for a long time," Nellie Birdsong declared, proudly displaying a piece of soft, white, home-tanned deerskin.

Ella Bone Necklace fingered the leather with a wrinkled brown hand. "Eee, that's nice. You've got good teeth."

Erin glanced at the younger woman's handiwork, giving the chubby baby in her arms a chance to tangle his fingers in her hair. Finger by fat finger, Erin worked to free herself as her curiosity got the better of her. "Good teeth?"

"The old way is best," Ella explained. "Soften with the teeth."

"But that new dentist at the clinic *really* gets after me every time," Nellie wailed. "I try to tell him this is the way my grandmother taught me, but he says he's gonna have a workshop next month that'll cure all my bad chewing habits."

"You mean you actually *chew* . . ."

"They had that workshop *last* month," came the comment from the far corner. Lily Count Coup seemed absorbed in her quilt pattern, contributing her information without looking up. "They show you how to pull string through your teeth. I told them we've been using sinew."

Erin looked from one woman to another. No one cracked so much as a smile. "But it would take weeks to chew a hide that size." Tentatively she looked to Ella for confirmation. "I mean, wouldn't you have to . . ."

"You'd have to work those jaws pretty hard," said a masculine voice at Erin's back. She turned to find that Hunter had managed to invade the feminine domain without so much as a warning sound on the steps. Her pulse rate doubled as, smiling, he walked toward her. "The Lakota woman who says her steak is tough as shoe leather knows what she's talking about."

The baby squirmed in Erin's arms, and she mumbled a strangely shy, "Hello, Hunter," as she set the little one down.

"Getting some tanning lessons?" Hunter wondered.

"I don't think I'm up to the challenge," she admitted, dazzled by the contrast between his dusky bronze skin and the pale-blue knit shirt he wore. "Anyway, I think modern technology has come up with ways that are easier on the teeth."

"Easier on the teeth, maybe, but not on men's ears. Indian men have always known that a woman with a mouth full of deer hide can do little complaining." Hunter tossed a conspiratorial wink at the woman with the hide. "I don't know why the white man thought he could improve on that method."

"Indian women have always known that men who loaf around the women's circle are the ones who don't keep their kettles full," was Nellie's dust-dry comment.

Hunter raised a palm in total surrender. "No offense, ladies, but I don't have time to chew the fat with you." The hoot from the corner was Lily's. Hunter replied with a good-natured shrug. "See what I mean? That's progress for you. If you'll buy me a cup of coffee, Erin, I'll put your name in print."

A bit red-faced, but still smiling, Erin glanced back at Ella, whose return smile, though mostly in her eyes, was thoroughly warm. "If you'll promise to leave out the part about chewing the fat," Erin said, preceding Hunter down the steps. One of these days she'd get over being a babe in the woods.

No matter what the weather, the drink here was coffee, strong, black and generally lukewarm. By midmorning Erin had always had enough of it, but everyone else took it all day long. It was late afternoon, and Erin brought coffee for Hunter and ice water for herself to the table in the corner of the dining room, where he sat waiting for her.

"Did you get your windows fixed?" she asked, smoothing the skirt of her bright-yellow sundress as she sat across from him.

"Yeah, but I'm still hassling with the insurance company over new rates. They want to call me high risk."

Erin raised a brow in complete agreement. "How's your arm?"

He glanced down at the inside of his forearm and the remnant of the injury he'd all but forgotten. "Good as new."

"I take it our sharpshooter has not been found."

"Not yet, but they're working on it."

"It's been three weeks."

"Three weeks" hung in the air between them like a cloud. Three weeks since they'd seen one another. Three weeks since they'd shared a night's terror and a moment's passion. Three weeks of wondering what the other was doing, thinking it best not to wonder and then wondering again. The look they gave each other now set wondering aside. It had been a long three weeks at Brave Wolf Publishing, just as it had been at the mission.

"Sounds like three weeks was long enough to get the ball rolling here," he said. "I'm doing an article on the project. Marlys has been filling me in. Even after cutting through her high praise and eternal optimism, it sounds like you've got something here."

"We will once the catalog is circulated. I left a message with Bernie to remind you...."

"I got it." He'd been there when she'd called, but she hadn't asked to speak to him. Just as well, he'd thought. "I brought along several printing bids. Did Marlys ever decide how big a print run she wants?"

Erin knew he'd called once to ask Marlys that question. Marlys said he'd asked about her, though he hadn't asked to speak to her. Just as well, she'd thought.

"We're still not sure. I'm applying for grants through two sources: the national church and the federal government. We should have some answers by the time we have the layouts done."

He lifted a shoulder as he set his coffee down. "It doesn't matter. I got bids on several options."

"We've already got several beautiful pieces to feature, and more in the making. I've been keeping an eye out for good settings. I've got some great ideas for pictures using some of the local color. The church bell, for instance. Did you know they brought it out here from somewhere back East, and it fell in a river on the way out? They had to dredge it out of the drink with a team of horses."

As he watched her brighten he let one side of his mouth curve in approval. She'd always been taken by the romance of the area's past. Twelve years ago history had interested him about as much as a plate of liver. She would insist on poking through the weeds to read epitaphs on the tombstones up on the hill, when all he could think about was that they were alone for a few minutes, and he wanted her in his arms. Now he shared her interest in the local color and, yes, he knew about the bell, but it was fun to listen to her tell about it and watch her eyes turn a deeper shade of green as she talked. An occasional nod from him was sufficient to keep her going.

"We can mention some of these things in the copy," she was saying. "No dissertations, of course, just brief items of interest, sort of playing up the mystique of the place. The flavor of the past along with the color of the present."

"Mystique? Interesting choice of words," he said, mulling the word over in his mind, examining connotations. "That's a word I'd use to describe some place like...Byzantium. Mysterious, exotic...a curiosity."

"But you can't really call it Byzantium anymore," she pointed out as though he needed a little instruction. "That's history."

"Exactly. Like I said, a curiosity. That's why we get so many curiosity seekers around here. It's that Indian mystique."

She detected a criticism of her in his tone, and she knew she didn't deserve it. Not this time. "I'm not a curiosity seeker. There was a job to do here, Hunter, and I was asked to help. I may not be the *only* person who could do it, but right now I'm the one who's available. I'm here, and I'm qualified. And things are going well."

He nodded. "I'm impressed with what I've seen. You've got something going here—no doubt about it. How long do you expect your interest to last, Erin?"

She folded her hands in front of her and leaned forward on her elbows. "This is Marlys's project, and Marlys will see that it continues. I'm pleased with the way it's going, and I'm excited about the prospects, but unlike you, I know I'm expendable."

"Marlys and I belong here," he said.

"By virtue of the color of your skin or what you have to offer?"

"Both. And also by virtue of a heritage that, for us, has very little to do with *mystique*."

Erin flattened her palms on the table in front of her. "All right, Hunter. I didn't pass the loyalty test. I know that. I've lived with that for twelve years, and for twelve years I've asked myself..." A quick glance into his eyes sapped her nerve. "I've wondered about many things, not the least of which is whether I can actually contribute...personally...to anything. Well, I'm here, and I'm contributing, and sooner or later maybe I'll be replaced by someone better suited to the job, but right now, I'm needed."

"Which one do you want to be, Erin? Needed or expendable? You've described yourself both ways." Even as he said it, he knew the description fit. He'd needed her, but he'd done without her, and he would again. The term *expendable* chafed in his craw, and he didn't know why. He'd proved to himself that it was accurate.

"I guess I'm in the same spot you occupied on the newspaper staff in L.A. I can do the job, Hunter. When I leave there may be twenty others ready to take my place, but it'll be a position I've created. I will have started something."

Her hands were clenched now, and there was a note of pride in her voice. It moved him. He wanted to say, Finish it, Erin. See it through. Show me and everyone else. But he only smiled, covering one of her hands with his, and said, "You're good at starting things."

They talked about the project then, Hunter assuming his reporter's role. It occurred to Erin more all the time that this was and wasn't Hunter. He attracted her the same way he always had, but he interested her in a different way. Time had passed, she thought, and while he'd taken on a hundred new facets, he saw her as unchanged. She knew she must have changed. In twelve years a person *had* to change. Hunter had gone to school, become a big-time reporter, probably romanced more than one woman, started a business. What had she done? Finished school and married Arthur. Period. Oh, she'd taken more courses, gotten her master's degree, done some charity work—nothing earth-shattering. He'd grown. Had she?

After the interview Hunter stayed for supper at Marlys's invitation and then decided to take a ride. Erin heard leather slap against leather and a quiet, "Ho, Gambler," as she approached the barn door. Under the brim of his light straw cowboy hat Hunter looked across the top of the saddle, and their eyes met. After a leisurely survey of her body from head to toe and back again, he quirked a straight, black eyebrow. Unlike too many women who wore them, Erin was built for jeans.

"You changed your clothes," he observed.

"I thought maybe you'd invite me along for the ride."

"You're invited."

He handed her Gambler's reins, took another headstall from a peg on the wall, and soon had his other horse, the big sorrel, in tow. Erin ducked out the barn door with Gambler, who was her sentimental favorite. She rode him around the corral to limber them both up while she waited for Hunter.

At her back Erin heard, "Lookin' damned good there, lady." Gambler took the corral corner at a trot, bringing Erin around to watch Hunter swing up into the saddle without benefit of the stirrup. He gave her a slow grin from his perch in the saddle.

Erin tossed a yellow-gold hank of hair back off her cheek and laughed. He knew exactly how to impress a lady. "You too, cowboy."

"You're in a saddle this time. Anything goes," he warned.

"Challenge accepted. Anything goes."

Hunter set the pace, gradually stretching everyone's limbs with an easy gait. They took a familiar route, first along a gravel road and then across rolling hills, where the grass was fading from green to yellow with summer's too-quick passing.

The land called up memories in Erin's mind, memories she'd thought had disappeared with the passing of time. Over there were the buffalo berry bushes they'd raided, eating most of what they'd picked. Here was the lone tree with the horizontal branch that Hunter had used as a chinning bar. Ahead was the draw where he had coaxed her down from her horse, stuck a pasqueflower behind her ear and then kissed her senseless. Remembering how hard he'd felt against her and how hot he'd made her feel brought the warmth washing through her even now. She leaned forward in the saddle.

She remembered, Hunter thought, his eyes narrowing as he watched her register each of their personal landmarks. She remembered with her body and her mind, just as he did. Her body was softer now, her hips no longer boyish, and the breasts that bobbed with the horse's trot had filled his hand just weeks ago. Without warning, he shifted and clucked for a canter. The sorrel wanted to run. Run, then, damn you, Hunter thought. Run!

Erin followed, not without fear at first, but the wind felt good and the freedom even better. Straightening her shoulders, she shook her fear loose and left it trailing behind, and she flew. Ahead of her the big sorrel stretched out and sailed across a narrow crevice. Gambler followed suit, and Erin gripped the saddle between her knees and rode the wind. On Gambler's legs she could outrun fear and failure and maybe even time.

Later they walked the horses, the silence still heavy between them. "You don't think I can do it, do you?" Erin finally asked him.

"Do what?"

"See this project through." When he didn't answer she added, "I understand your doubts about me, Hunter, and I understand your suspicions of outsiders. But I'm doing something important for a change, and it feels good. It isn't what I came here for, and I didn't think it would come to much at first either, but now..." She looked over at him, wanting him to be convinced on her word alone. "It's going to work, Hunter. I know it is."

He tilted his hat to shade his eyes and slanted her a speculative stare. "Why did you really come back?"

With a sigh she admitted, "I'm not sure anymore. Mostly for Louise."

"To find out who killed her? That doesn't cut it, Erin."

"Why not?" she demanded stiffly. "Why shouldn't her murderer pay for what he did?"

"Nobody said he shouldn't pay. But you've got no more chance of finding him than I have of carrying that boulder home." She followed his gesture with her eyes and noted the huge jagged rock embedded in the side of the hill they were passing. "So why are you here?"

She considered and offered a slight amendment. "Mostly *because* of Louise. My little sister. She thought she was following in my footsteps when she came here, but she was really blazing her own trail. She did what I lacked the courage to do."

"And what was that?" Hunter asked quietly.

"I knew a certain feeling when I was here before, a feeling I haven't known since I left." She felt the intensity of his stare, and she hastened to add, "A feeling of purpose. Louise had the same feeling, and she followed it up with a commitment. I think she lived for something, and I think she died for something. I want to know what that something was. I want a piece of it."

Hunter swung his dark gaze to the east, and the pale white moon stared down at him. A certain feeling, he thought. She didn't even know what it was. No wonder she couldn't deal with it. No wonder she'd married the wrong man. The right credentials, the right address, the right skin, and the wrong man. A feeling she hadn't known since she left, was it?

"Oh, look, Hunter, it's one of those sunsets. We used to laugh about riding into the sunset. Just like this, remember?"

He turned in the direction of her voice and watched the sun ease itself into a pocket between two buttes and leave a painted sky behind. "A South Dakota sunset. Believe it or not, it's been setting the same way for the past twelve years."

She chose to ignore the sting. "And look at the moon! It's almost transparent. Where else in the world can you see the moon and a sunset like this both at the same time?"

He shrugged. "Wherever the land is flat and the air is clear." She was looking back and forth, trying to keep both orbs in view, and he decided to stop bombarding the moment with sarcasm and add to the magic instead.

"We have a legend," he began, "that says the sun and the moon were once forbidden lovers. The Old Ones, who ruled before man's time, discovered the two together, and they were cast to the heavens in opposite directions with the earth always between them. Only during the brief moments when day becomes night and when night becomes day are they allowed a glimpse of each other."

The horses slowly picked their way down a gradual slope as Hunter's eyes sought Erin's. "There's beauty and sadness in the moment. Each strains to see the other, but the distance that separates them is immense, and the whole earth stands between them."

Erin's heart was trapped in her throat, and her first words were raspy. "Do you think...after all this time, do you think they still love each other?"

"I think they will always love each other."

Hunter stopped the sorrel and swung down from the saddle, inviting Erin down with a look. She saw then where they'd come. They were near a train bridge, its trestle spanning the river, which ran summertime slow and easy. She closed her eyes and smelled the pungent sage, remembering the time they'd crossed the river on the treacherous catwalk that ran under the bridge. His hand on her thigh reminded her of the intimacy they'd shared under the bridge that day. When she opened her eyes she was lost immediately in his. She slid down into his arms, meeting his kiss with her own before her feet even touched the ground.

He kissed her deeply, and she sank into the warm depths of his mouth. When it ended she was shaken, and he knew it. There was satisfaction in knowing it. "It hurts like hell to be too far away even to touch," he said, his voice a soft rumble.

"Yes, it does."

"But even if all you get is a brief glimpse, you take it. You take it because you can't turn away."

"You don't have to turn away," she whispered.

He smiled. "You dropped the reins again." She looked down, and he showed her that both sets were in his hand. "When are you going to learn, Erin O'Neill?"

He tied the horses to two fence posts along the railroad right-of-way, and then they slipped through the barbed wire fence, Hunter stretching the wire apart to allow easy access for Erin. Taking her hand, he led her to the seclusion beneath the trestle because they both remembered, and the memory had quickened each one's pulse many times since.

"You didn't much like that catwalk, did you?" he asked. The grass was tall here, and their boots blazed the trail as the grasshoppers sprang out of the way.

"It terrified me."

"Why did you cross it with me?"

She remembered clinging to him, the joints in her knees turning to water, but he'd gone, and she'd followed. "As I recall, it was on a dare."

"Is that what it takes? A dare? Did I dare you to let me make love to you?"

"No. As I remember I said, 'Not here,' and you said, 'Erin, this is the best I can do.'" They were underneath the bridge now, and they paused near a rock so large that Erin was able to prop her backside against it and remain standing.

"But you were afraid then, too."

"I was always afraid of making love with you, Hunter. I was afraid of the consequences. I was afraid of the way it made me feel. You were too good at it, and I thought for you it must be . . ."

"Must be what?"

"Must be easy. Must be . . . practiced, I guess. But you were the first for me. After that, there was only Arthur."

Hunter clamped his teeth together. He didn't want to hear about "only Arthur." Besides, he hadn't been good at it then. Surely she must have realized that by now. He'd wanted her desperately, and he hadn't been able to take the time to make it really good. Now he knew what he should have given her, what he could give her, what he wanted to give her at this moment, as their separate orbits brought them within reach once again.

Tossing his hat to the ground, Hunter leaned toward her, bracing his arms against the rock behind her, enclosing her on all sides. He used the pearl-black sheen in the depths of his eyes to hypnotize her. The effect was apparent in the guileless look on her face. Without quite letting their bodies touch, he lowered his head, bending his elbows until his lips reached hers, and then he worked them slowly, giving small, soft kisses, moving with her responsive mouth and teasing with his tongue.

The heating coil in the pit of her stomach began to glow. His control made him all the more enticing, but she sensed an underlying dare. His kiss invited brassiness, his tongue tempting some bold gesture on her part. She let her hands pave the way by finding his waist. Deepening kisses honed her nerve, and she tightened her grip and pulled him firmly against her. He sank his fingers into her hair and his tongue into her mouth and let her show him what she wanted him to do.

She explored his tapered back and the muscles in his shoulders that bunched under his knit shirt as he hunched over her. But she wanted him to fan the heating element that made such a golden glow inside her. Her hands slid slowly down his back to tuck themselves into the back pockets of his jeans and hold him fast. He felt his whole body smile. With a steady rhythm he pulsed against her.

With a groan he released her mouth and peppered hot kisses over her flushed face, making his way to her ear. "This isn't all you want, is it?" he asked, his voice grating against the back of his throat.

She swallowed convulsively, looking for her own voice. "No."

"No, what?"

"No, it isn't all I want. I want more, Hunter."

"More games, Hunter?" He nipped at her ear. "Or more of Hunter?"

"Much more of Hunter," she breathed, curling her fingers against the hard muscles of his buttocks.

"I want more, too, honey. But not here. I can do better than this now."

"It doesn't matter. I'm not..."

"It does matter." He straightened, taking her shoulders in his hands and pulling her away from the rock. Surprised, she dropped her hands to her sides. "How much more of me do you want, Erin? Do you know?"

"I think so," she said, shaken by the hard glitter in his eyes.

"I think *not*. Do you want me in your life, or just in your bed? Do you want me for three months? Six? Have you given it much thought?"

"I haven't..."

"No, you haven't. You still haven't figured out that feeling you were talking about—the one you said you haven't known since you left here." He would have none of her head-shaking. He clamped her head between his strong hands and made her look at him, made her listen. "That feeling had nothing to do with a place or a project or any mystique you care to name. It has to do with *me*. It's been there a long time, Erin; I think it's about time you figured out what it is."

"I told you how I felt about you. I told you, and I gave you . . . everything."

"And then you took it back. Erin . . ." He hesitated, surveying her face as his thumbs crept along the delicate line of her jaw. His eyes softened. "I want more of you, too. I want you lying next to me, naked, on cool sheets. I want to fill you with my seed, and I want the right to hope it takes root inside you. I want to fall asleep with my hand on your belly and wake up with my face against your breast."

She closed her eyes, and he heard the catch in her breathing. "That scares you, doesn't it?" Her chin dipped once against his hand. "Hell, it scares me, too. It always has. But you said something about commitment. Louise knew the meaning of that word. She knew it well. I know what it means now, too. But I wonder whether you ever will."

She jerked her head back, and he let her go. "You're so sure of yourself, aren't you." It was an accusation, not a question. "You don't care what the risks might be. You know you can deal with them. Don't you know what our relationship meant to me, Hunter? Don't you realize how much of myself I gave you, and what it took to make me give you up?"

"No, I don't," he said quietly. "What did it take?" She shook her head and tried to move away, blinking furiously at her tears. He snatched her shoulder, pulling her back. "What did it take, Erin? Did someone force you somehow?"

She shook her head furiously, muttering, "No, no. It was my decision."

He detached himself from her slowly, taking a deep breath and a step back. His jaw was set, his eyes suddenly devoid of emotion. "It's getting dark," he said. "We'd better get back."

# Chapter 6

Brenda Chase adjusted the flowered print arm covers on the chair in Erin's little office. There was a squeak of overused springs as the young woman shifted uncomfortably, watching her own fingers smooth the fabric and then readjust it. Sipping her ice water, Erin watched the slender brown fingers, too, and waited patiently.

"I don't like him anymore," Brenda said in a small voice. "He's mean, and I don't want to live with him anymore."

"Are you ready to leave him?" Erin asked.

"I can move back in with my mother."

Moving in with her mother meant Brenda would probably be back with her husband within a week. "There's a place for you here as long as you need it," Erin reminded her. "Give yourself some time."

Haunted eyes darted Erin's way. "I don't want to make no trouble for him, though. No cops."

"That's your decision. If you want to sign a complaint, I'll go with you. If not, we'll leave it at that."

"I don't." The arm cover needed attention again.

In a few short weeks Erin had become a better listener than she'd ever thought she could be. She didn't blink an eye at a black eye or a bruise anymore. Brenda's less active hand was sprained. Erin made no judgments. She offered a profusion of options, but little direct advice. There was nothing smug about her attitude. Not even to herself did she say, "If anyone ever did this to me, I'd..." Instead Erin listened, and she empathized. The first thing a woman in trouble needed was a place to go—safe, neutral territory. The last thing she needed was an "I told you so."

No man had ever struck Erin—not Arthur, not her father, not anyone. But how many years had she suffered Arthur's mental abuse, and how much had she returned in kind before she'd said enough is enough? He'd suffered her furthering her education, but he'd refused to cooperate with her efforts to get a job. She'd finally allowed herself to slip into a role that left her feeling useless with a man who left her feeling cold. He'd suggested many times that she'd never really left Hunter, and she'd often wondered if that were true.

What had it taken to make her give him up? She knew what had come to Hunter's mind immediately when she'd posed the question and he'd thrown it back at her. He assumed it was money, social status, the security in choosing "her own kind," as her father had so carefully phrased it. In the end she'd opted for security. And in the end the only "I told you so" came from her own heart.

Young and very much in love, she'd gone home full to the brim with the happy knowledge that Hunter was everything that excited her in a man. Still, she had to admit that he frightened her, too. He was at loose ends in his life, a free spirit, terribly reckless at times. He'd offered few promises: a roof over her head, food on the table and a bed to share with the man who loved her. She'd left South Dakota in September thinking that was all she wanted. Within a few months she'd heard all the arguments from all the well-meaning friends and relatives, and she'd begun to doubt that it could be enough.

You come from two different worlds. The passion will cool, but the differences will always be there. You'll begin to resent each other. Where would you fit into his life-style? What about children? Does he want them? Can he provide for them? Would they be Indian or white? You could destroy the man, Erin. He'd end up hating what you are, and you'd begin to wonder what you ever saw in him.

What had it taken to make her give him up? Her soul, she decided. That was why she'd been dead inside all this time, and that was why she'd come back. Part of her needed to be rebuilt.

Brenda Chase needed to rebuild, too, but she was afraid. This was the touchy stage—making the break. Erin remembered how many times in her own marriage she had thought about it, examined the words, practiced saying them. That was the crossroads, the place where Brenda stood now. She needed to start asking herself questions like what do I have, and what do I want? The mission refuge would give her the opportunity to look for answers, if only she would give herself the time.

"We have a policeman living on the premises now, Brenda. Perry Trueblood and his wife have the apartment in the boys' dorm. You don't have to worry about anyone coming after you."

"Once he cools off he'll realize what he's done and he'll be sorry. He always is." Brenda glanced up quickly to show Erin that her own resolve was still intact. "Won't do him no good, though. I don't have to take no more of that, do I?"

"No, Brenda, you don't." Don't do the "forgive and forget" number on yourself too quickly, Brenda. Forgiving isn't easy, and forgetting is nearly impossible.

Another quiet moment passed. "He got laid off. He was working construction. First job he'd had in more than a year. He's better when he's working."

"Does he love you?"

The young woman hung her head. "I don't know."

"But you love him." Brenda nodded. There was the rub. "Would he agree to counseling? Not necessarily with me, but maybe with someone else?"

Brenda lifted her chin, wide-eyed. She was lovely, Erin thought. Dark hair, slight build and troubled eyes. "Oh, no. He'd never do that. He'd never...if he knew I was telling you all this, he'd..."

"This is between you and me, Brenda. And just between you and me, I think your husband is going to come looking for you, hat in hand. When he comes, let's let Father Wilkins talk to him."

"Gary won't talk to Father Wilkins. He won't even come to church."

"He will if he wants to see you." Erin smiled. "And I think he's going to want to see you. He'd be crazy if he didn't."

"He is crazy. Sometimes I think he's just plain crazy." But the twinkle in Brenda's eye told Erin that keeping the woman from going back to her husband before morning wouldn't be an easy task.

Hunter hung up the phone and added little touches to the doodling on the pad in front of him. PAN-INDIAN LIBERATORS. His block letters were perfectly square, perfectly neat, and the words made him see red. If this were an American group, we'd probably call them the PILS, he told himself with a wry smile, and that seemed to be exactly what they were. Sam Whiteman had a lead on somebody who fit Rick Morales's description, and he wanted a picture.

The Liberators were an elusive bunch whose members, Latin American dissidents for the most part, had been insinuating themselves into American Indian communities wherever they thought they could heat up a little trouble and bring it to a full boil. Their cause, they said, was Indian unity, but they seemed to promote only dissension. Claiming to be from any reservation other than the one they were on, they were known to attack progressive Indian leaders as well as non-Indians, and they were not above employing terrorist tactics.

CRIMSON EAGLE. Hunter traced the letters, saying the words to himself in Lakota. *Wanbli we śa.* Treaty rights was the issue. It had begun as a peaceful attempt to make a statement about treaty rights. Outside influences were muddying the issue. These so-called liberators came from places where governments toppled monthly, and people were "educated" at gunpoint. Here we have our disagreements with the federal government, sure, and we voice them, he told himself. But these people, these liberators, had no idea what a free press was supposed to be, and they obviously didn't like his. He'd had enough trouble convincing the Tribal Council what he was about. He didn't need some lunatic fringe from south of the border sitting up on the hill taking potshots at him.

Would they have had a reason to take potshots at a church worker, too? Crimson Eagle was the kind of activity the Liberators looked for, but why would they have targeted somebody like Louise, somebody who was completely apolitical? Sam had helped get a couple of Liberators put away for a while, but he said it was hard to get much out of them. They were fanatics. Who could figure a fanatic?

Hunter tossed the pencil down and leaned back in his chair. A folder caught his eye. The printing bids for Erin's catalog. *The mission project's catalog*. Why had he said Erin's? Probably because he'd been tasting Erin's mouth and feeling the pressure of Erin's hips ever since.... He stood up, shoving his hands in his pockets, and looked out the window. Nice day, he thought. Might be a good day to take pictures of quilts and church bells.

"You look lovely!" Marlys stepped back for a full-view appraisal as Erin came into the kitchen.

"Just a clean pair of slacks," Erin declared with a shrug.

"A change of clothes in the middle of the day." Taking a walk around Erin, Marlys made an inspection. "A very recent shower, hair washed, scent of...some kind of flowers, I'd say." She'd reached the front again. "A little extra mascara, and, yes, a definite hint of eyeshadow. When's he coming?"

"Come on, Marlys, it's hot out. I was wilting."

"Will he be here for supper?" Marlys persisted.

Erin capitulated with a roll of her attractively accented eyes. "I don't know. He's coming to take some pictures for the catalog. He said about two o'clock."

"We'll make him stay for supper. That's all I can do, Erin. The rest is up to you."

"Marlys, this is not a campaign."

"No? Then why the perfume?"

Erin tried to suppress a grin, but it showed in her eyes. "Because I like to smell good. Even for you."

Hunter was at the door of Erin's office promptly at two. The droning little fan that swept back and forth across the room pretending to be a breeze overpowered other sounds, and when she looked up to check the time there he stood, filling the doorframe. A brown leather camera bag dangled from one hand, and the ever-present cowboy hat was in the other. Erin's last lungful of air seemed stuck in her chest. Hunter made jeans look like something tailored just for him.

"You're right on time," she said, as though the fact might be noteworthy.

"Habit I picked up off the rez."

Filing away some papers, she glanced up and smiled at his use of the local expression. Life on the reservation did not revolve around punctuality. She shoved the desk drawer to its usual sticking point and then leaned back to work at it from a different angle. "This...darn...drawer...is stuck."

"Here, let me give you a hand. Looks like a B.I.A. desk." He moved behind her, and the scent of masculine cologne tickled her nose. Its woodsiness complemented her flowers.

"You mean warped?" she asked, smiling at the secret notion of dovetailing campaigns.

He got the right leverage on the stubborn drawer and gave it a hefty shove, sliding it closed. "Not really. Just stuck dead center."

"But it usually works from eight to five."

Hunter slanted her a grin over his shoulder. "Or eight to four-thirty, if it only gets thirty minutes for lunch."

Erin grinned back, enjoying the fact that she was up on the joke. Anything that didn't work smoothly was attributed to the Bureau of Indian Affairs, which was noted for its plentiful supply of red tape. "I hope that's not a government surplus camera you've got there."

Slinging the bag over his shoulder, he swept her an "after you" gesture. "This here's a genu-ine Japanese import, ma'am," he drawled. "Brave Wolf Publishing's own. So break out the trade goods and let me hear about some of these great ideas you've got. I've got an invitation for supper if I finish this up by five-thirty." For Erin's benefit he added, "From the padre's wife."

They left and got started on the pictures.

Hunter followed Erin from "great idea" to "fantastic idea," enjoying the ever more excited expressions that accompanied her description of each setup. They used the old bell, which sat on the ground in a big weathered timber frame. Below the bluff the mission sat on they scoured the lazy curve of the riverbank. There, amid the graveyard of river bottom trees, they found just the right arrangement of bleached-white driftwood. Whole trees that had washed ashore, their ghostly limbs reaching into the cloudless blue sky, made wonderful places to drape the traditional star quilts for Hunter's photographs.

A forgotten harrow and an old single-bottom plow, both weathered and nestled in tall, wind-rippled grass, served to display beadwork and home-tanned hide. They used a squaw cooler in several pictures; the homemade shady spot, a shelter of willow branches that was a summer tradition in many Indian yards, created an interesting play of light and shadow on blankets and beadwork. Gambler even managed to get into the act by modeling a beautiful beaded breast collar across his thick barrel chest.

"There's more," Erin announced after she'd exhausted her pile of handmade wares. Hunter dropped another roll of exposed film into a can, hiking a brow in disbelief. "Carol Walks Alone has designed beautiful appliquéd skirts and vests, but they aren't ready yet. I have to find models for those, and for the men's Western shirts with the appliqués and the starbursts in the yokes." She gave him a coy smile. "Want to volunteer?"

He gave her a wary look. "No way, lady. You need me *behind* the camera."

"But you're so perfectly... proportioned."

He could feel the heat from those bold green eyes as they swept his body from head to toe. Hooking an arm over her shoulders was a face-saving gesture. He thought he might be blushing, though he figured he could count on his deep tan to conceal any such foolishness. "There's nothing more tempting than a high-class hussy," he mumbled, giving her shoulder a squeeze as they headed back toward the dining hall. "My proportions could use a little sustenance."

"I have it on good authority that we're having fried chicken," she informed him happily, settling an arm around his lean waist.

"Mmm, my favorite."

"The good authority knows that. Apple pie for dessert."

"That should take care of the perfect proportions." He grinned at the prospect.

Supper reminded Marlys Wilkins of the nightly excitement she'd enjoyed in years past in the dining hall. Several women and children were present, some crafters, some seeking refuge. The program provided meals that could be earned or purchased inexpensively. Since the closing of the boarding school Marlys had missed the children and the constant activity. It felt good to let the voices drift around her and know she'd taken a step toward putting this long-standing institution to good use again.

Watching Erin and Hunter turn shining eyes on each other across the table was like old times, too. Erin's refined femininity was the perfect foil for Hunter's dry-witted teasing. They related their afternoon's accomplishments like a practiced team, one playing off the other. Oh, they would make such a good pair, Marlys thought. They'd forgotten themselves, letting the empty years roll back just for the moment, and it showed on both their faces. The only problem was that neither of them had seen it yet.

Hunter pushed himself away from the table and patted his flat belly as though the food he'd just put away showed. "Well, padre, I think I'll ride fence for you tonight, work off some of these pounds. It's a lonely job, but somebody's gotta do it." The look he slanted in Erin's direction was one she remembered. It meant, *You're coming, too*.

Managing to gather a stack of dishes before anyone else had a chance at them, Erin headed for the kitchen, announcing over her shoulder, "I think it's my night for KP."

Marlys shook her head over the second cup of coffee. "How many times have I told you, Erin? That's not your job." She turned an exasperated look at Hunter, as though he'd somehow missed her point.

With a reassuring wink at Marlys, Hunter took his plate and followed Erin. "Hey," he said when he caught up to her at the sink. "Just a ride this time, okay? No bridges. Let's backtrack a little bit."

"Backtrack?" She eyed him warily. They'd spent a nice afternoon together, and she didn't want to see it spoiled. She'd come away from the last ride with a deep-down ache.

"Sure. Start out fresh. First date." He grinned down at her worried expression. "No kissing on the first date, as I remember."

She gave him a tentative smile. "Right."

"I was afraid I had that right. Damn. I hope I can remember all those lines about sunsets and taking you for a walk to the moon."

"I hope you can think of some new ones." Her smile was more secure now.

Marlys appeared in the kitchen doorway, frowning. "Hunter, will you get this woman out of my way so I can get cleaned up here? She's used to an automatic dishwasher, and she's as slow as my Aunt Minnie."

Hunter nudged Erin out the door, advising, "Don't argue with the padre's wife. She knows some words, let me tell you."

The ride that night was everything Hunter had promised—no bridges, no kisses, no talk of the past. Erin talked about her work at the mission, and Hunter listened with an open mind. Hunter talked about his interviews with several attorneys, including the state's attorney general, concerning the issue of water rights on reservation land. Erin was interested in the intricacies of state, federal and tribal law, and the process of sorting out the three. From Erin's point of view it ended all too soon.

Two nights later she came down for supper and found Hunter washing up in the bathroom at the end of the kitchen hallway. He turned to grab a towel and caught her smiling at his dripping face. Once again, the years dropped away.

"Hi." His grin was boyish, his eyes bright.

"Hello." Her smile was sweet, her eyes flirtatious.

"I noticed some fence down the other night. Just came out to fix it."

She took note of his clothes—well-worn jeans and a faded red Western shirt, one he might easily have had when he was cowboying years ago. "Carter will appreciate that, I'm sure."

He took a swipe at his face with the towel. The hair around his face was damp. "Think his ol' lady will appreciate it enough to feed me again?"

"There's nothing out there anymore but your horses, Hunter Brave Wolf, so you oughta fix it." Marlys poked her head through the door and shoved a pan of cornbread under his nose. "Take a whiff of that."

Hunter obeyed and offered a predictable "Mmm."

Drawing the pan back, Marlys challenged, "Now, who's an *old lady*?"

Flashing his irresistible grin, Hunter slipped an arm around Marlys and swore, "Your Aunt Minnie."

"Set another place, Erin."

It was good for both of them, this fresh start of Hunter's. He was right. They needed to backtrack, to let all the disappointments fall by the wayside and find the very beginning of a thread that had become tangled over the years, but had never broken. Erin anticipated evening rides with Hunter several times a week, and Hunter planned his days around them. The conversation between them was easy, the laughter rich, and the long looks and electric touches became promises without words.

"Where's our hungry newspaperman tonight?" Marlys wondered one evening, dragging up a chair beside Erin's desk. "He doesn't usually miss dinner three nights in a row."

"I think he's worried about his figure," Erin offered without looking up. Her attention was fixed on the circle of light under her desk lamp. "You're notorious for trying to fatten men up."

"What are you working on?"

"Copy for the catalog. Hunter thinks we can start working on the layouts. It's going to be beautiful, Marlys. He's a wonderful photographer." The look in Erin's eyes, now that they were turned Marlys's way, said there were any number of words that could be substituted to Erin's satisfaction for "photographer."

"Is it going to work out this time, Erin?"

Marlys wasn't one to beat around the bush, and Erin didn't pretend not to know what she meant. "I don't know. Some things have changed; others haven't. Whether it's the right combination of changes remains to be seen."

"You've changed, you know," Marlys said.

It was a feeling Erin needed to have confirmed. "How?"

"The way most women change over the course of that first decade of womanhood," Marlys said. "You've learned to deal with reality. I think you see what's important now and what isn't."

"Hunter's changed, too," Erin said thoughtfully. "He's less cocky and more careful."

"He's more courageous, Erin. You have no idea the courage it takes to do what he does, to say things that need to be said even though sometimes no one wants to hear them."

"He reminds me of Louise." Erin smiled wistfully, remembering her sister. But the smile clouded. "Hunter respected Louise—admired her commitment. If she hadn't been married already when she came here..."

"Uh-uh." Marlys cut that thought off with a shake of her head. "Never would have happened. Louise was a lovely person, but she wasn't you. And you, my dear, have deified her beyond anything she'd appreciate."

Erin sighed. "Her death was so unnecessary."

"Her death was not your fault."

"I know that." There was a vacant expression in Erin's eyes, a sense of unaccepted loss. "She always had to follow me. I used to think she was such a pest."

"She came here because it was in her to come here," Marlys said, her voice lacking any hint of pity. "She was way beyond acting on the inspiration of her older sister, so you can get that grand thought out of your head. What's done is done. You have your own commitments to think about."

"I have a commitment to Louise," Erin said flatly. "Beyond that, I'm still testing the waters."

"Testing the waters? Ha!" Marlys wagged a finger in Erin's face and flashed a smug smile. "You're already in over your head, young lady. You're just too stubborn to—"

The conversation was interrupted by bounding footsteps, followed by Reverend Carter Wilkins's appearance at the office doorway. His voice was calm, but his expression was grim.

"There was a fire in the newspaper office tonight. I don't know the extent of it, but Hunter's been hurt."

## Chapter 7

Father Wilkins's Suburban barreled over rutted back roads like a Sherman tank. Erin gripped the dash, twice asking whether the big wagon could go any faster. Finally, shoulder to shoulder, Erin and the priest marched into the small McLaughlin clinic as though they'd come to do business. They were turned away. Hunter Brave Wolf, they were told, had been treated for burns and released.

"Well, thank God," Erin breathed, turning a relieved expression in Father Wilkins's direction. "He must not be seriously hurt."

"I wouldn't say that." The nurse's interjection brought both heads around. "He refused admission. We told him those burns were nothing to sneeze at, but he wouldn't stay."

Shoulder to shoulder, the two marched out again.

Brave Wolf Publishing seemed to be intact from the outside. Erin saw little evidence of damage as the Suburban rumbled past the building, but it was nearly dark, and the smell of smoke hung in the evening air. The windows of the house were dark, too, but Hunter's car was parked in the driveway. Except for that and the dog's barking, she wouldn't have thought anyone was home.

Beating Father Wilkins to the door, Erin rapped a fist, rang the bell and called Hunter's name all at once. After a ten-second pause, she barged in. The shape of a man in a corner chair was just discernible in the dusky living room.

"Hunter? It's Erin. Father Wilkins is with me."

It sounded so much like a line from a movie that Hunter actually found himself laughing. His mind's eye saw her approaching his deathbed with eyes brimful of pity and a tear-jerking farewell on the tip of her tongue. "There's nothing wrong with my eyes" was his dour return.

"We heard you'd been hurt." She couldn't see much, but just the sound of his voice was reassuring.

"You heard right. I'm not in a great mood for—"

The table lamp was clicked on, and a distinctly feminine gasp followed.

Hunter turned his face from the glare. "Oh, geez. You didn't have to bring her here tonight, Padre. She never could stand..." Rolling his head in her direction again, he found Erin kneeling beside the arm of the chair and staring at the bandages on his arms.

Having assumed a Sphinx-like pose, he'd been making every effort not to stir too much. He was fairly numb, and he wanted to stay that way. But Erin was hurting for him. It showed in her face. "It's not as bad as it looks," he said finally, the urge to comfort her winning out over the urge to growl. "Just a bunch of gauze."

"I had no choice but to bring her here," Carter Wilkins said. He stood awkwardly by the door. He was accustomed to rushing to the scene when someone was injured, but obviously this was Erin's time. "Now that I see you're not in need of last rites, is there anything I can do? Anything *else* I can bring you?"

Hunter frowned at the little smile lurking under the priest's shaggy red beard. Wilkins had brought more than enough. Hunter didn't think he was up to handling Erin right now. More to the point, he wasn't up to handling himself around her. "Erin, go on home," he urged quietly. "I'm okay."

"You're not okay. You're badly burned, and you should be in a hospital."

"What you see here is just a pile of bandages. They got a special deal on gauze this month, and they're using it generously. All I need is sleep."

"You won't get much sleep tonight," she promised him. "I managed to get some hot-oil burns once. I know what it's like." Craning her neck over her shoulder, Erin found Father Wilkins standing with his hand on the doorknob. "I'm going to stay, Father. The nurse told us this man should have been hospitalized, and I have a feeling what's under these bandages is pretty grim."

"This man's temper's about to get pretty grim," Hunter mumbled. "I prefer to do my suffering alone and in the dark."

"You'll have to throw me out, then."

Hunter glanced down at his gauze-wrapped fore-arms and back up at Erin's determined face. "I find myself at an awkward disadvantage."

"Look, I'm not needed here. I'll offer up my prayers for the loser in this argument on my way home." Father Wilkins saluted Hunter with a parting thought. "A little TLC never hurt anybody, Chief."

"Neither did a little peace and quiet." Hunter raised his voice on the last words, but the door shut anyway. "Thanks a lot, Padre."

Erin lowered herself onto the hassock at the foot of his chair, sank her chin in her hands and gave him an innocent look. "What's with the big protest? I'm here to wait on you hand and foot. I promise, you'll love it."

"Oh, yeah?" He raised a booted foot from the floor. "Then how about starting with my feet."

Taking each foot between her legs and working the heel of each boot loose she managed the chore with a pleasant smile. "What else can I do to make you comfortable?" she asked.

"Well, now, let's see." A challenge was in his tone. "I generally sleep nude. Think you can help me get that way?"

"Certainly. Are you ready for that now?"

"Are you?"

She gave him a very sweet smile. "Think of me as your nurse tonight, Hunter. In that sense I'm completely at your disposal. Whatever I can do for you..."

"You can give me a little sex to dull the pain." His eyes glittered, and she knew he was only half kidding.

"If you're still trying to run me off, it won't work. Did they give you anything for pain?"

"They gave me some pills, but I haven't taken any." He dropped his head back against the chair, closing his eyes.

"Shall I get some for you?" He rolled his head from side to side. "Would you like a drink, then?" That brought the same reaction. "Is this what they call 'toughing it out'?" she asked.

"Remember that time I got hung up on a bull at the Little Eagle Rodeo?" he asked, his eyes still closed.

"I remember very well." She'd choked back a scream and nearly suffocated. "After they got you loose you wouldn't let anyone touch you. You had to walk out under your own steam."

"And then I had to get behind a horse trailer so I could break out in a cold sweat and black out without anybody seeing me. After that I needed time to cuss a blue streak and limp around a little. And that's what I need right now."

"Feel free," she said, shrugging. "Some patients prefer pills, others profanity. Whatever works best for you is fine with me. Have you eaten?"

"Hell, no."

"And you're hungry."

"Damned right I'm hungry, but—"

She cut him off with a silky, "Good. I see the profanity's working. You have an appetite. Something easy on the stomach, I'd say. And something quick." Her eyes brightened at the obvious choice. "An omelet?"

"I don't want to eat."

Her hand on his thigh sent a warm ripple throughout his body and changed the tone of the conversation. "Eat, Hunter. The pain gets worse later."

"I know."

The skin on his forearms felt tight and hot, but he knew the real pain hadn't set in yet. Nature gave the victim a short respite. His hands were okay, and the fire hadn't licked much above his elbows. He decided to give in and let her feed him. What the hell—might as well get something out of all this. She seemed to get a kick out of playing the nurse for him, and he didn't have to lift a finger.

A little while later he sat in the armchair in the living room, letting himself be fed like some kind of invalid, and concentrated on those green eyes. There was some kind of soothing elixir in those eyes.

She figured he'd need water. Sick and injured people always seemed to need a lot of liquids, and she offered it until he rebelled. "Enough! You're going to float me away, for God's sake." She backed off, and he apologized with a wry smile. "Do you know what kind of problem a simple zipper's going to give me tonight?"

"None," she said without looking him in the face. "I'm here to alleviate ... problems like that." She offered a tentative smile. "As your nurse, of course. Nothing personal."

He returned the smile, but there was nothing tentative in it. "I only wear one zipper, honey, and it's about as personal as you can get."

Setting the empty plate aside, she cut him a flippant glance. "It's all in the attitude."

"Mm-hmm. And yours is too damned saucy for a nurse. Even a night nurse." He liked the sound of that and gave her half a grin to prove it. "Even a *private* night nurse."

"If you weren't such a pathetic sight, Hunter Brave Wolf, I might feel threatened."

"It's going to be a long night." The heat under the bandages was getting worse. He settled back in the chair. "Aren't you going to ask me what happened?"

"I thought you'd tell me when you got ready." She wasn't sure she wanted to hear. The teasing was a brave front. She hated seeing him like this, and she'd been pushing back all thoughts of the fire that had done this damage to him, threatening his life.

"My office was firebombed."

"And you were in it?"

He shook his head. "I was working in the darkroom. I got to it in time with the fire extinguisher, but I guess I got in too close. Some of those pictures for the catalog were sitting out on the desk, and I . . . well, I lost them."

His fingers, curved over the arm of the chair, were a dark contrast with the white bandages. As though she thought he might be tender everywhere, she carefully placed her fingers over his, matching them one to one. "Hunter, you didn't get these burns trying to save some silly pictures, did you?"

"They're damned good pictures, but I still have the negatives. I guess it was just a reflex." He'd admonished himself later for trying to dodge the flames to reach those pictures, especially when his editorial for this week was sitting right there beside them, and he didn't have a copy of that. Sheer stupidity. But he knew those pictures were the only things in the office he associated with Erin. Funny how you react in a no-thought situation, he told himself. And in a situation like this, with her so close and touching only his fingers...

"Do you think it was the same person?" she asked. "The one who shot at us?"

"Probably."

"Do you have any ideas?"

"Some."

"And you've discussed them with the police."

"Of course." He'd discussed them with Sam Whiteman in L.A.

"This can't go on, Hunter. We've got to do something."

"We do?" He chortled, raising a brow at her ingenuous indignation. "What do you suggest, Nancy Drew?"

"Hunter, this is not funny. People can't just go around doing these things. If the police won't do their job you've got to talk to the Tribal Council. Surely they don't want to see this newspaper go up in smoke."

"Maybe we could call it *Smoke Signals*."

"Hunter!" The way he grinned just with his eyes could be infuriating.

"You're right. I think it's been used."

"Hunter, I'm very serious. You always seem to delight in close calls, but they're a little hard on my nerves."

"Are they, pretty paleface? Is that why you..." No, he didn't want to ask that. Not now. He wanted to touch her, but when he lifted his free hand lightning shot through his arm. After a midair hesitation he let his fingers find the smooth plane of her cheek. "I love it when you're 'very serious.'"

Her fingers tightened on his, and she shivered under the tenderness of his touch. Her eyes drifted shut, and she whispered, "Hunter, I'm scared."

"I won't... let anyone hurt you." He had to lower his arm, set it back carefully on the arm of the chair. It was killing him.

"You've let someone hurt you." The anguish in her eyes was not for herself. "Look at you. If you'd been sitting at your desk, working late as you often seem to..." For want of being able to hold him and be held by him, she leaned forward and dropped her head on his thigh. "I'm scared for you, Hunter. You're hurt, and I hate that, but you could have been ... This time it was too close. You can't shrug it off."

He was sitting there with Erin's head in his lap, for God's sake, and his arms felt as if they were going to fall off. He decided he was about to find out which was his lower threshold, pain or passion. "I'm not shrugging it off. I'm very serious, too." He shifted in the chair a little. "In fact, by the time this night's over, I'll probably be ready to take scalps."

She lifted her head. "Whose?"

"Not yours, though I'm sure it would make a nice trophy." With her hand on his knee, her scoop-neck summer top offering a hint of the swell of her breasts as she leaned forward from her perch on the hassock and that wide-eyed concern she was giving him, she had him convinced that her trophies were myriad. The fact that he was up to his elbows in burns and bandages didn't make them seem any less desirable. If she didn't back off pretty soon he was going to pounce on her, bandages and all.

"Do you think it's someone who doesn't like your editorial outlook?"

"Mmm, I think that's a good possibility."

"Who?"

God, Erin, he thought. If those green eyes get any wider, I'm going to dive into them and cool off. "I think I'd like something cold . . . to drink. Whatever you can find."

"Of course," she said quickly. "You're not feeling feverish, are you?" Leaning closer, she cupped both hands around his face. His thick black hair reeked of smoke. "I'm not sure what kinds of side effects . . ."

He inhaled her wild-flower scent and dug his fingers into the upholstery. "I'm not sick, Erin," he said, pulling the stops out on patience. "I'm a little thirsty, and you looked like you needed . . . something to do."

Withdrawing with a twinge of embarrassment, Erin took a step back from the chair. "I'll see what's in the refrigerator."

She brought him a soft drink, and he insisted he could handle it and took it in one hand. "Sit down, Erin, and we'll talk until one of us falls asleep." She started for the hassock, but he flicked his chin at a chair. "I should have said, 'Have a chair, Erin.' I feel like I'm expected to keel over any minute." She sat. "Now," he began, "what do you want to talk about?"

"Suspects. Let's make a list of people who don't like you," she suggested.

"That should cheer me up. You want this week's list or last week's?"

"Oh, for heaven's sake, Hunter, you can't be that unpopular. Everybody knows that a newspaper has to be unbiased except where the editor is called upon for an informed opinion.''

He smiled at her naïveté. ''Everybody knows the good guys wear white hats, too. We're not talking small-town politics here, we're talking Tribal politics. In the past the Tribe has owned the paper, and I mean literally. They hired the staff, and there was no criticism. You could lambaste the Department of the Interior and the memory of George Armstrong Custer, but never a councilman, never the local government and never touch the cousin or brother-in-law of anybody who's anybody. So you're left with covering school basketball games and praising local programs. And absolutely nothing to read.''

''You've changed all that,'' Erin noted.

''Damn right. It took me a year to show people what a free press actually meant, and another year to persuade them that I wasn't—couldn't be—on anybody's side. But I'm still not radical enough for the activists, or traditional enough for the Council. No matter how many times I tell them that all I do is observe and report, they still want to know what I'm up to—whose side I'm on.''

''You're saying you're not really trusted?'' He'd been something of a local hero in the days when he'd rodeoed. How was it possible to lose that regard after leaving home and becoming successful? ''But you're from here. They know you.''

''They *knew* me. I lived on the outside for a while, came back with some fancy ideas.'' He smiled at the thought. His own printing press was pretty fancy. An economically sound business in the hands of an Indian owner was very fancy.

"You don't think anyone . . . any of the Tribal leaders would . . ." Her gesture indicated the damage to his arms.

He shook his head. "No. If somebody around here doesn't like what I have to say, he comes and tells me. Then we argue, call each other a few names, all face-to-face. This coward's approach isn't the way we like to do things."

She thought he was probably being a bit optimistic, but she hoped he was right. Still, somebody out there didn't like him, and somebody had disliked Louise enough to kill her. Erin knew that she was as frightened for Hunter as she would be for herself. He should have been more suspicious, she thought, of *everybody*. On her next trip into the kitchen she locked all the doors.

"I was working on the copy for the catalog tonight before . . ." Erin sat down at the end of the couch nearest Hunter's chair. His face was drawn, his lips pressed tightly together. Keep talking, she told herself. "Before we heard about the fire. I think it's going to be wonderful, Hunter. Everybody's anxious to see it printed."

"I'll get some more prints, and then we'll get together on layouts as soon as . . . in the next couple of days." The flesh under the bandages had gone white-hot. The initial reprieve was about over.

"Maybe we could work on the layouts tomorrow. You can instruct me, and I'll do the work. That way we'll get an idea what size—"

"We'll see." The words came more abruptly than he'd intended.

Erin moved to the hassock and sat by his knees again, her eyes full of sympathy. "What can I do, Hunter? How can I help?"

He managed a smile. "You can keep right on talking about something else and ignore me if I bark at you. Tell me about your end of this project. How's the counseling business?"

For his sake she brightened. "I think I'm pretty good at it. I know I've gained confidence in myself, and I'm gaining trust. We had a non-Indian woman come in the other day. Her husband is quite prominent in Mobridge, and she was terrified someone would find out that she'd sought help. She talked for quite a while and then left, but I think the next time it happens she'll come to us."

"What do you do about the men? Do you report them?"

"We leave that up to the victim. We tell her what her options are. If she decides she's going to go back to him, we try to get her to stay with us until the man involved, generally a spouse, is willing to talk to Father Wilkins. Hopefully we can get a dialogue started."

"Is it working?" he asked.

"We've just gotten started, but I think the indications are promising. We've been accused of meddling, and we've had some angry guys pounding at the door, but we have a policeman on the premises now. You know Perry Trueblood."

"Two-hundred-and-twenty-pounds-of-muscle Perry Trueblood?"

"That's him. He moved into one of the apartments, lock, stock and weight bench."

"Nobody argues with Perry," Hunter acknowledged. "I thanked him for the last speeding ticket he gave me."

"I thought you said you didn't speed anymore."

"I don't. I wasn't. Perry said I was, and like I said, nobody argues with Perry. So you're safe." He slouched back in the chair and dropped his head back, eyes closed. "I'm glad. It's a good project, Erin. A noble effort. You'll leave here with a real eagle feather in your cap."

Leave here? She hadn't thought of that in weeks. "It was ingenious of Marlys to combine the two projects."

"With good management it'll work. That's always the hangup. That and—" he turned his head in her direction and opened one eye "—good counseling. We've gotten some lousy advice around here."

"A good counselor isn't one who's dazzled by his own advice." It felt good to be able to say that, knowing for the first time in her life that she was a professional counselor and that she could be good at it. But she was new to it, too, and a little self-conscious about that fact. She shrugged, dropping her gaze to Hunter's closest knee. "Anyway, relationships between men and woman are much too complicated to be able to just hand out a sheaf of advice."

"How can a woman stay with a man who deliberately..." It was something he hated so much that he found it difficult to say.

"Women want to be loved," Erin said. Her voice became hushed, hurt. "It sounds simple and so obvious. We want love. But since love isn't a thing that someone can hand you in a box and say, 'Here's my love,' we're not always sure when we're getting it and when we're not. I've seen too many women lately who believe that a man shows his love with the back of his hand.''

"Or with the size of his bank account?" Erin glanced up, and he caught her eyes with his. "How do you want to be loved, Erin? What are you looking for?" It was part of the question he kept trying to bury, but it kept bobbing to the surface in his mind. Why didn't you come back to me, Erin? Didn't I love you the way you wanted to be loved? Was I too demanding, too bold? Did it frighten you to know how much I wanted of you then? Knowing how much more he wanted her now, even with the pain he felt and the pain she might offer later, he turned away from her struggle to answer him.

"I'm looking for something in myself." She spoke softly, hoping to squelch the tremor that threatened her voice. "I thought if I found the right man I could sit back and let him make me happy. It didn't work. Now I have to find out what I have to offer."

"Men want to be loved, too."

She found that he was looking at her again, his eyes turned smoky brown. She tried to return the message without getting misty, but the tears welled in her eyes. She'd hurt him, she knew that, but she'd never stopped loving him.

"It sounds simple and so obvious," he echoed, his voice turning husky. "A man doesn't ask for love easily. He may demand it. He may declare it. But asking a woman for love is next to impossible for a man."

"A woman should be able to give without being asked." The tears stung her throat as she spoke, but the words wanted out. "Without conditions. Without a list of expectations. I think when a woman knows what she has to offer she can accept a man's love for what it is. It doesn't have to come to her in a name-brand box."

She needed to be touched, and he needed to touch her. No amount of pain could have kept his fingers from her face. "I think when a man loves a woman properly he lets her know what she has to offer."

One tear formed at the corner of her eyes and hurled itself over the edge at the blink of a lash. He caught it on a gentle forefinger and then tipped her chin up to meet his lips. There was pain in their kiss. There was the sting of regret and the salt from old tears. But mostly there was hunger—hunger for the end to pain and regret and tears that another kiss could bring. With her hand against his cheek she offered to take his pain. He groaned into her kiss, dropped his trembling hand and brushed his lips over the crest of her cheek to take her tears away.

"I'd show you tonight, Erin," he whispered into her hair. "I'd show you right now, but I did say *properly*." He dropped a kiss into the part in her sun-yellow hair and slumped back into the chair, shaken from his efforts. The seared skin beneath the bandages screamed.

"Will you take something for the pain now?" Erin asked gently. "You said they gave you a prescription."

"No. I don't think those pills will help much." He gave her half a smile. "They'd probably make me as wild as whiskey does, and I'd rather keep my head on straight. What I'd like is a cigarette."

"Come to think of it, I haven't seen you smoke." He hadn't been a heavy smoker, but she remembered him reaching for a cigarette after a rodeo or when he was with other cowboys. And she remembered the few times when he'd gone bar-hopping with his friends; she hadn't been invited along. He'd always been unapproachable for at least a day after one of those excursions.

"I gave up all the bad habits," he told her, reading her thoughts. "But I picked up some cigarettes on my way home from the clinic in honor of this...occasion. I left them on the bureau." A flick of his head indicated the back of the house.

"I'll get them for you."

The cigarettes were in plain view on the bureau in what was obviously Hunter's bedroom. The room looked like Hunter, with its navy blues and rusts, its oversize bed, serviceable oak furniture and Western prints on the wall. She had turned to leave when a framed photograph caught her eye from the nightstand. It was small, but she recognized it immediately as one she'd given him long ago.

"I'd forgotten about that."

His voice startled her. Reflexively, her head jerked toward the doorway. She felt as though she'd pried, and she flushed with the embarrassment of it.

Actually, that picture wasn't something he kept on display, but it had always been close by over the years, tucked in a drawer. He'd be looking for the mate to a sock or down to his last T-shirt, and he'd discover it, and all the memories would come rolling back as they had the other night, when he'd taken it out and studied it for a few moments. He'd asked himself what in

hell he was going to do about the persistent feeling he
had for this green-eyed lady. For some reason he
hadn't put the picture away, but there was no point in
explaining all that now. It would sound like an ex-
cuse. "For old times' sake," was all he said. "Did you
find the cigarettes?"

"Yes," she said, holding up the pack.

Feeling light-headed, he leaned a shoulder against
the doorjamb and watched her inexpertly tear into the
package of cigarettes, skirting the bed as she approached him. "There's a spare bedroom, and a spare
toothbrush in the medicine cabinet. I'm assuming you
didn't come prepared to spend the night."

She gave her head a tight little shake. "But it really
isn't necessary."

"That's what I said, but you wouldn't listen. I'm
fresh out of nightgowns, but I do have an extra robe
hanging on the back of the door in the hall bathroom." With a stiff arm he made an attempt at pulling the snaps apart on his Western shirt. Irritated by
his own clumsiness, he lost patience and gave the shirt
an ineffectual tug.

Erin set the cigarettes aside and went to help him.
With her hands over his, she glanced up, and he par-
alyzed her with a heated stare. Then slowly, one by
one, she undid the snaps as he lowered his arms, never
releasing her eyes. Her heart pattered against her ribs.
Slowly, and with great care, she pushed the short-
sleeved shirt over his shoulders. He winced as he
shrugged out of it, letting her guide it over his throbbing arms. His chest was silken, bronze and hairless.
She remembered what a sensuous pillow it made.

Pulling away from the hold his eyes had on her, she dropped the shirt, which smelled of smoke, into a hamper near the bedroom door. "Sit down before you fall down," she suggested. "I'll get you a cigarette."

He stood where he was, the hooded eyes following her every move as she managed to extract the cigarette, put it between his lips, strike a match and light it for him. He drew on it, squinting past the smoke. With the cigarette dangling from his mouth he looked like a thug. A delicious shiver accompanied the thought that he looked tough, that maybe he was just a little bit dangerous. The thought, she realized, was an old one, and the shiver recurred.

"You really should go to bed," she told him. "You don't look well. Shall I..." Her eyes fluttered over his jeans and back up again. "Do you need help with..."

He took another deliberate pull on the cigarette and then plucked it from his mouth, saying nothing, his eyes giving her no quarter. Swallowing hard, she unbuckled his belt and unthreaded the leather strap. She glanced up, and he smiled when the hands that reached for the snap of his jeans brushed against his belly.

"That's enough." His voice was almost guttural. "I'll keep my jeans on. I just want to lie down for a while. I won't sleep. Think you could find me an ashtray in the kitchen cupboard?" When she left the room he let his breath out slowly.

She hurried back with the ashtray and a glass of water, and found him sitting on the edge of the bed. His face was ashen, and the eyes he lifted to her were bright with pain. She knelt beside him and peeled off his socks. "I brought you some aspirin. Surely you can't object to simple aspirin."

Accepting without comment, he swallowed the aspirin and drank the whole glass of water. Then he handed her the glass, lifting one patient brow. "I took those to get rid of *your* headache. Feel better?"

"I wish I could do something, Hunter. I wish I could . . ." She lowered her eyes, feeling foolish.

"Kiss it and make it better?" He sent a cloud of smoke over her head. "I wish you could, too. In fact, I think my original suggestion was the adult version of that cure. Maybe we could compromise. Forget the spare bedroom and just lie here next to me. I promise you, I'm perfectly harmless." He crushed the cigarette in the ashtray.

"I might not be. What if I bump against your arm?"

"I'll risk it."

They lay there in the dark next to each other on his bed. She didn't dare touch him, but she felt the heat from his body. He couldn't reach for her, but he was comforted somehow by her presence. He knew the moment when she finally succumbed to sleep, and he stopped counting the minutes and concentrated on the sound of her quiet breathing.

It was still dark when Erin awoke later and realized that Hunter was gone. She felt the depression his head had made in the pillow next to hers and smelled the smoke that clung to him still. Tomorrow I'll wash his hair for him, she thought as she rolled off the bed. His hair and . . . whatever else he wants washed. If she couldn't take away the pain, at least she could make him a little more comfortable.

She crept into the hall and heard the ragged edge of his breathing. The sound tore at her heart. She found him lying on the living room floor in a patch of moonlight, his arms draped over his abdomen, and she dropped beside him. "Hunter, what ... my God, what are you doing on the floor?"

"Go back to bed, Erin." The low voice was carefully controlled.

"What are you doing in here?"

"I'm standing behind a horse trailer reliving every eight-second ride I ever made. I'd like to do it without an audience."

She saw the telltale sheen across his face. When she touched his forehead he rolled his head away. Her fingers came away wet. "I don't mean to sound...inhospitable...Erin...but please go away."

She did, but she was soon back. "Maybe it'll help to elevate them. Here, let's try."

He let her cover him with a blanket, sliding it under his armpits, and slip a thick cushion between his abdomen and his arms, but he grumbled. "I wish you'd just leave me alone. I've got a few filthy words ... I haven't used yet."

"You've also got some painkillers you haven't used yet." She knew he was chilled. She tucked a blanket over his shoulders.

"You mean the sex? Parts of me are still willing ... to give that a try."

"I mean the pills. Please try them, Hunter."

"Erin," he said evenly, "my arms are on fire. My nerve endings are raw. Those pills will leave me nauseated and still hurting like hell. Now go to bed. Let me get back to my cussing."

With a damp cloth she began swabbing his face. "Cuss away, cowboy," she said softly. He groaned.

"It'll be all right," she promised. "This is the worst of it. It'll get better tomorrow."

"Tomorrow we try sex," he mumbled.

"We've tried it before," she whispered. "Remember?"

"Yeah," he answered, letting his mind drift. "Worked damned good." Her voice was soothing. The cool cloth on his face was soothing. He closed his eyes and pictured her naked. That was soothing, too. "Erin?"

"Yes."

"The blanket hurts my arms."

She folded it back, exposing the awful bandages again.

"Erin?"

"I'm here."

"Thanks for staying . . . this time."

## Chapter 8

Hunter wasn't sure whether the pain had abated in the past twenty-four hours, or whether he was just getting used to it. He felt better if he didn't move around much. When he reached, he felt as if his skin was ripping apart. Erin had insisted they visit the clinic, where the nurse who changed his bandages seemed to take sadistic delight in declaring how awful his arms looked. Seeing the blisters on his own raw-looking flesh was bad enough, but hearing her graphic descriptions had nearly made him sick. It had taken several deep breaths of outdoor air to clear his head.

There were calls from the Wilkinses, the police, the insurance company and several calls from Bernie before Erin finally took the phone off the hook. After lunch Hunter had agreed to take more aspirin for her headache, and then he'd finally been able to sleep for a while. When the burning woke him, he lay there and studied the swirl patterns in the ceiling until he could drift off again.

Marlys dropped off some clothes for Erin and stayed only long enough to hear Erin's version of the firebomb story and a description of Hunter's condition. After she left, Erin took up the washing she'd promised herself she'd get done. Hunter's smoky clothes and anything else that looked dirty went into the washer. She also tossed in the slacks and top she'd slept in the night before.

From the window she noticed that Bernie was overseeing the cleanup of Hunter's office. One comment she'd overheard him make on the phone that morning had, in fact, irritated Erin just a bit. "Go ahead, if you're sure you don't mind. You're the only one I trust in there, Bernie. You know my office as well as I do."

Okay. So Bernie was cleaning up his office. Erin was laundering his pants. Big deal. Once the laundry was taken care of, Erin fed Blondie, whose habit of jumping into Hunter's arms had gotten her relegated to the backyard. The dog growled, and Erin returned the warning. The females in Hunter's life definitely did not want her around. Finally she decided to pamper herself with a shower, a feminine summer top made of sheer batiste and a generous amount of the cologne Marlys had thought to include with her clothes.

It was evening when Hunter wandered into the kitchen like a sleep-logged adolescent and announced he was starving. Erin fed him all he would eat and insisted that he drink a second glass of water, explaining that the clinic nurse had agreed on the benefits of extra liquids.

"The old biddy enjoys other people's pain," he grumbled, setting a third glass away from him. "She wants to see if the biggest blisters she's *ever* seen can blow up any more before they bust wide open."

"Well, we'll just save it for later. Are you ready for your bath?"

Hunter looked askance at her, his eyes danced, and a slow grin spread across his face. "I'm sure I couldn't manage it myself."

"And I'm sure that breaks your heart." With a hand on one hip, she gave him a sassy smile. "I thought I'd wash your hair in the kitchen sink first. It got a little singed on the ends."

"Really?" He reached up, but she was standing over him, her hand already there, and he deferred.

Four fingers plowed deep furrows in the coarse black thatch over his forehead, drawing their way through to crinkled ends. "With a decent pair of scissors I think I could take care of this for you."

"Have at it, then. There's a pair in the desk drawer."

She slipped her hand into the hair over his temple and smoothed one slightly singed eyebrow with her thumb. "I don't know about these, though."

"What about them?"

"Obviously you haven't looked in a mirror." Her snicker invited his frown. "You look sort of wild."

"I *am* sort of wild." The palm near his face got a playful nip to prove it, followed by a soft-lipped kiss. "But wildlife experts say I can be tamed."

His breath tickled in her hand. "By what means?"

"By a green-eyed lady with a decent pair of scissors." He grinned and flashed her a wink.

"Let's get you washed up, then, and give it a try."

His hair was easily taken care of. Hunter complained about bending over the sink, but he cooperated. Bare to the waist except for the towel that hung over the back of his neck, he sat more patiently for his clipping. Erin's deft use of the scissors removed all traces of fire damage. When the job was done he gave her that slow smile again. She'd promised him a bath.

"Of course, there *are* several options here," she said finally.

"Let's go over them one by one."

"Well, let's see, there's—"

He took hold of her wrist, tugging steadily. "Why don't you have a seat?" He nodded, dropping his eyes to his thigh, and she settled there. "Now, the options?"

"Well, there's the traditional cat bath," she began.

"Your tongue or mine?"

"The expression refers to..." Taking note of his bemused expression, she decided, "That probably wouldn't be suitable." He turned his mouth down and shook his head. "Then, of course, there's the bed bath."

"Hmm."

"They give those in the hospital to bedridden patients," she explained, smiling along with him now.

"But I'm not bedridden."

"No, you're not."

"You know, I'd really like a nice warm, relaxing tub bath." He made it sound like something to be coveted. "But I don't want to get my brand-new bandages all wet."

"You could keep your arms out of the water."

"Yes, but I really feel grimy." He was the model of chaste innocence, both in tone and facial expression. "I need to be washed with soap and water. All over. By someone who understands what I'm going through. Someone who really—"

"I promised you a bath; I'll give you a bath." She shrugged, smiling sweetly. "No big deal. I'll run the water."

She helped him get undressed, and that *was* a big deal. Try as she would to keep moving matter-of-factly from one thing to the next, Erin's hands and eyes gave her trouble. She wasn't sure what to do with either. For Hunter, it was all delightful diversion from the nagging pain his burns caused him. He understood why clowns and comedians were welcome visitors to children's wards.

About the time his jeans hit the floor, he laughed. "You've just gone from a pretty paleface to a blushing redskin, Miss O'Neill. Relax. You've seen it all before."

"Well, I haven't exactly... stripped it all down before." She made a project of folding his clothes.

He chuckled. "No." She heard one leg plunk into the water. "I did all that for you." A second plunk in the water. "You were pretty flushed then, too, as I remember." A soft slosh. "But that was before you became a private nurse and took on this unabashed, clinical attitude toward my body, which is now covered..." She glanced at the tub, and he grinned. "With clear water."

"Maybe the water will turn black from the soot," she mumbled, taking the soap from its dish.

"You should be so lucky." He watched her as, at once blushing and trying to suppress a smile, she lathered a bath sponge and mounted a vigorous assault on his shoulders and chest. "Take it easy, Miss O'Neill. I'm an injured man. Lack of consideration for my... delicate condition... could bring on some side effect that might be... mmm... difficult to deal with." The circular motions of the abrasive sponge over his chest were invigorating. He settled back, smiling, his arms resting along the sides of the tub.

"You'll go down teasing, though, won't you?" she accused.

"I don't think you have to worry about my going down." Closing his eyes, he told himself to enjoy, muttering, "The side effects will be quite the opposite, I'm sure."

"Give me a leg," she instructed, lathering the sponge some more. The lather that had spread from his chest to the water gave her a reprieve.

"Leg," she repeated, pretending exasperation when he hesitated. "Yours. Up, out of the water."

"One leg, coming up." The water sheeted down from his leg as he lifted it for her. It was long, lean, muscular and several shades lighter than his chest. "Did I ever tell you the joke about Three Legs, the intrepid Sioux warrior?"

"No, and I don't think I want to hear it now, either. Other leg."

"Right. That's the punch line."

Erin gave in to a sputtering giggle and tossed the soggy sponge in his face. "You're about to get your mouth washed out with soap, *injured* man," she warned.

Leaning toward her, he sought her indulgence with smiling eyes. "Not before you scrub my back, I hope."

She started on his back with the sponge, but with his appreciative groan she set the sponge aside and massaged the soap over his slick, wet skin with kneading palms and undulating fingers.

"Oh, God, that feels good."

"Do your arms hurt very much now?"

"Nothing hurts now, hon. Not a thing."

"Good," she whispered. "That's good."

Minutes later, when he came out of the water, there was no teasing and no awkwardness, only lingering, heated eyes and unsteady breathing.

Wordlessly, Erin took a towel from a rack and began drying Hunter's body. He suffered the long, slow strokes with the towel as every one of his muscles pulled itself taut. He'd known for some time that he would make love to her again, but he'd planned to give it the full extent of his efforts. Now, here he stood, every cell in his body aching for her except the ones in his arms. They wanted to wait a while longer.

Her blouse had gotten wet. The thin, soft cotton had become transparent over her lacy bra, revealing the outline of nipples that had hardened at the sight of him and at the feel of him under her hands. Her chest rose and fell with each breath. The towel fell from her hands, which she lifted to the smooth curves of his pectoral muscles. His small nipples reacted, just as hers had. The cells in Hunter's body took a quick vote. The majority ruled.

Hunter dropped his head forward and nuzzled her neck with warm, wet kisses. She closed her eyes and shuddered, letting her hands roam at will. His skin was damp satin, and she needed to touch it everywhere. He lifted his arms but couldn't pull her to him, and that was fine. She wanted to touch him, freely and easily. She wanted to slide her hand along his back and over the hard curve of his buttocks, so she did. Her pulse fluttered wildly. He took her mouth with a deep, urgent kiss, and her heart thudded in her throat. But she wanted to touch him more, much more.

The long line of his waist and hip felt both cool and hot—cool from the window's breeze, but warmed by his own heat from beneath the skin. As Hunter tilted his head to reposition his mouth over hers, Erin sucked in a breath and moved her hand to the front of him. With a groan he covered her mouth with another hungry kiss. His hard need filled her hand, and she massaged it much as she had his back, with firm, even strokes meant to give him some measure of satisfaction.

Distantly, the back door rattled beneath an insistent knock.

"Oh..."

"...no."

The raspy protests came from two stiffened bodies. Another pounding at the door assured them of the unwelcome reality.

"It'll go away," Hunter hoped.

They heard the door open, followed by a female-sounding, "Hunter?"

Erin's eyes widened. She extricated herself and flew to the bathroom door. She eased it shut, then grabbed his jeans and held them out to him, mumbling, "I think it's coming in."

"Go see what she wants," he implored breathlessly, stepping into the jeans she held up for him.

"She's *your* right-hand man," came the reply through clenched teeth.

"Go on!"

"Would she walk right in here, too?" Erin asked.

"Give me a break, Erin. I need ... thirty seconds." He lowered his eyes, and hers followed. Oh. Yes. Perhaps it would be best if Erin greeted Bernie.

Bernie had a budding reporter's eye. She noticed Erin's wet clothes immediately. She was also possessed of some discretion, and she decided not to ask Erin if she'd been watering the lawn. "How's Hunter?" she inquired instead.

"Well...he was hurt quite badly." Erin pushed her hair back with one hand. As always, Bernie filled out her crisp sundress admirably. "But you know Hunter. He's a hard man to... keep down."

"Is he—" Bernie inclined her head and gave a concerned frown "—in bed?"

"Oh, no," Erin said quickly. "He's, uh, he'll be right out."

Hunter appeared, managing a convincingly haggard expression. "Hi, Bernie." He'd also managed nothing more than the jeans, and he looked sexy and decidedly male.

"Oh, Hunter, you poor thing. Your arms! How's it going?"

"It's a royal bitch, Bernie, let me tell you." He dropped into a chair and threw her a doleful look. "Ever been really burned?"

Very little escaped Bernie's notice, and Hunter's fresh-from-the-bath appearance was noted as a corollary to Erin's damp clothes. Hunter had always struck Bernie as a man with a woman in his past. Obviously, this was the woman. "No, but you have. I can see that. It must hurt terribly," Bernie offered sympathetically.

Hunter shrugged, unthinkingly trying to offer an open-handed gesture and wincing when the effort pulled at his tender skin. "Not as bad as it did last night. The hell of it is, it hurts when I talk. What's up?"

"I took pictures of the office before we moved anything, and then we started in cleaning. We'll need new carpeting, chairs—the desk should be replaced. We lost a camera and some files. That white powder from the fire extinguisher was all over everything, along with the soot, but we salvaged a lot. I used up a lot of vacuum cleaner bags, but I cleaned up the files. I don't know how we'll get rid of that smell."

Hunter flashed a grin at Erin. "What did I tell you? This woman is amazing."

"Yes. Right there when you need her."

Hunter swallowed a chuckle. He knew he'd have to play this scene with studied grace. "I damned sure need her now if I'm going to get a paper out this week. I want it out on time."

"I have copies of most of what was on your desk," Bernie told him as she assumed the chair across the table from him. "How about the editorial?"

"I'll have to rewrite that, along with an account of the firebombing. You'll have them first thing in the morning."

"I can—"

"You can dictate them to me, Hunter," Erin said, her offer slicing firmly through Bernie's. "I'll type them up for you."

"I can do that," Bernie got in on her second try.

Erin stood at the counter, just behind Bernie's chair. Hunter had a view of both women's faces at once as they looked to him to choose. It was an enviable position, one that amused him, and he savored it for a moment. This was a small thing, but women always attached great meaning to small things.

"I'm burdening you with enough responsibility, Bernie. I'll be in tomorrow, but you'll probably have to be my hands for a day or two. As soon as I can, I'll be paying some visits to some people." He noted a spark of interest in Erin's eyes. "I need to do some . . . special interviews."

"We'll meet our deadlines," Bernie promised.

"Good. I'm counting on you."

Bernie was satisfied. She left the house knowing that her boss had faith in her, and that she had a job to do. She also knew that when the woman from the East went back where she came from, Hunter would still be there. And so would Bernadette Barker.

"Now," Hunter began after the door had closed behind Bernie, "the obvious question is, where were we?"

"We were going to write an editorial, I believe, and something about the firebombing of your office. Paper and pencil?"

His face registered a combination of resignation and disgust. "In the desk."

They worked together on the article over several cups of coffee. They would digress from the work occasionally when a name or a word would bring something else to mind. Conversation between them had always come easily. Everything Hunter said seemed especially clever. All Erin's comments seemed fresh and insightful. Neither could bore the other.

Even their silences were good moments. There were long looks and warm smiles and thoughts of warm bathwater and soapy hands as they communicated only through their eyes.

The phone rang, and Erin answered it. "It's long distance, Hunter," she said as she handed the receiver over. She hadn't intended to, but she found herself eavesdropping when she heard Hunter report the firebombing to the caller.

"I can't understand why he'd come after me. Yeah, I know it's a lunatic fringe, but I can go up there and get one.... Sure.... No, I'm okay.... Not unless you want to donate some skin. I think we're about the same shade of ugly." Hunter laughed, and Erin imagined laughter at the other end of the line. "Look, Sam, send me all you've got on this one. He sounds like the one we've got up at Crimson Eagle.... Sure, I've got one, but I need one of those fancy holsters like you guys wear." More laughter. "No, it doesn't go with the press card. Listen, watch your tail, Sam. I'll get back to you."

Erin made no effort to disguise the fact that she'd been listening, and he felt her eyes on his back before he turned around. "Sounds like you've got some ideas," she said.

He shrugged. "Just a lead."

"And some plans?" she wondered aloud as she crossed the kitchen and came to him.

"I've always got plans."

He wasn't going to tell her much about the call. No point in pressing. "I wish you'd said that twelve years ago." She smiled and laid her hands on his chest.

"I had dreams then. Would plans have sounded better?"

"At the time it would have. Now I like the sound of dreams."

Draping his forearms over her shoulders, he touched his forehead to hers. "When are we ever going to get it together, Erin O'Neill?"

Her heartbeat took an irregular turn. "What are you planning?"

"I'm planning to seduce you, and I've been racking my brain for ideas. I've never tried it without arms."

"I'd have sworn you wrote the book on creative seduction."

His low chuckle was deliciously wicked. "I thought we'd gotten a good start on a new chapter before Bernie interrupted."

"Oh, that. That wasn't going to amount to anything."

At her smile he tipped his chin to facilitate a teasing little kiss. "No?"

She rolled her forehead back and forth against his. "It was just the standard treatment for burn patients. Water therapy."

"Water's supposed to put the fire out." He pressed his lips to her temple. "You were fanning the flames."

"You're entirely too combustible," she argued feebly. He was leaning against her now, and the heat from his body drew her closer to warm herself.

"Fire fighters like to use a back-fire. I thought maybe we could try it." He moved against her, impressing her with his need. "If we make it hot enough the fire on the inside might cancel out the fire on my skin."

"Oh, Hunter, that's ridiculous." She'd seen the angry flesh and the blisters on his arms herself, and she'd seen the blood drain from his face when they were exposed. "You can't possibly..."

"Let me try." His mouth came down slowly, covering hers all at once. Their tongues met, and Erin slid her arms around his waist and knew she'd let him try anything.

They moved to the bedroom, and Hunter watched while she removed first her sandals, then her slacks and top. It was a job he preferred to do himself, but it occurred to him that she offered a gift this night in a way she'd never offered it before—not to him. He had no feeling of being patronized or pitied for his injuries. He knew that she came to him as a woman, and he would take her as a man.

Covered only marginally in swatches of lace, she stood before his bed, bathed in moonlight. His stiff arms went to the snap on his jeans, but she eased his hands away and undressed him.

She smelled like spring. He nuzzled her ear, warning, "You're about to find out that some parts of me are still working."

"How well?" she asked, smiling into the darkness.

"For you, at peak capacity."

The gravel in his voice made her shiver as he planted a row of kisses along her collarbone. He used his fingers to push the straps over her shoulders, but his mouth did the rest of the savory job. Bending to her breasts, he taunted her through filmy lace with delicate nibbles and the delightful nudging of his nose and chin. When she could stand it no longer Erin pinched the clasp between her breasts, and the garment fell away. Hunter's lips and tongue were those of a man bent on bringing her exquisite pleasure. As she threaded her fingers in the luxury of his thick hair, she dropped her chin to her chest. She wished she could reach him somehow with her mouth, but then wishes became cloudy as sensation intensified.

His kisses trailed over her midriff, his tongue painting small swirls as he sank to his knees, and she gasped his name.

"That was a fine bath you gave me earlier," he murmured. "I'm returning the favor."

"I had . . ."

"Don't think about what you've had," he ground out. "Feel what I'm giving you."

"Hunter . . . Hunter!" Wishes flew to the wind. No wish had ever been this compelling. He knew what she wanted before she wanted it, and she soared on the wings of his name.

When he felt her deep quiver, he sat back in the chair that stood behind him, pulling her quickly to his lap. "Straddle me," he implored, his voice husky. "And then ease my way. I want to make love to you."

Hands would have been superfluous. Erin's arms went around Hunter's shoulders as she lost herself in his kiss. She lifted her hips to allow him passage, and the arrow of the hunter sheathed itself in the heat of secret flesh. Simultaneous groans, one low and guttural, the other soft and breathy, expressed joy beyond pleasure. Erin was no longer empty, and Hunter was home.

Later they lay side by side on Hunter's bed. Hunter was as still as the summer night's warm air. Erin's hands soothed his body, smoothing his skin like a treasured satin coverlet. He loved it—loved the very thought that she enjoyed touching him. There'd been a time when he'd done all the touching, all the soothing, given all the assurance that his intention was not to hurt her in any way. Tonight Erin comforted him.

"I've had nothing," she whispered suddenly.

"What?"

She rolled her lips over the curve of his shoulder. "Between Hunter then and Hunter now, I've had nothing else. I just wanted you to know that."

"You had a husband."

"And you had other women. Was it like this with them?"

"No," he admitted honestly.

"That's what I thought. When we...made love...I knew it was the same for you as it was for me. It was a feeling of being back where I belonged...with you."

He turned his mouth to her forehead and kissed wisps of hair along with her cool skin. "Why did you wait so damned long?" he whispered.

"Oh, Hunter," she sighed, "I wish it could have been as simple as you wanted it to be. I know I complicated it with fear and stubbornness and pride. So often, I wondered how you felt—whether you even thought about me after all this time."

"I thought about you."

"Seeing you again was wonderful...and it was so much worse than I dreamed it would be."

"Wonderful and *worse*?"

"So much had changed, and yet nothing had really changed. I felt the same way I did the first time I saw you."

"How was that?"

"Stunned."

"Stunned?" He was trying to remember the details of that first meeting, but he remembered only Erin— willowy-looking in her summer cotton skirt, which danced around her legs in the wind. He remembered the long blond hair, the fine-featured face and, when the dark glasses came down, the cool green eyes. Beautiful.

"You don't remember, do you?" she accused.

"Of course I remember."

"Where were we, then?"

He chuckled. "We were outside . . . somewhere."

"You were in the corral working with Gambler, and you wore a red shirt and a very battered straw cowboy hat, and you moved like thick molasses, taking your sweet time about ambling over to the rail to give me a taste of your 'Howdy, Miss,' with your world-famous disarming smile."

"No kidding? Pretty easily stunned, are you?"

She took a sliver of his shoulder between her teeth and pinched him smartly enough to make him yell "Ouch!"

"Never before had I been stunned," she informed him, "and only once since." A moment's pause was followed by the quiet admission, "When I saw you at Crimson Eagle."

"You surprised me, too."

"But you said you already knew I was here. Why were you surprised?"

"Because I was so damned glad to see you."

The confession made Erin glow internally.

Erin had gotten some sleep, but she knew Hunter hadn't, at least not until early morning. There'd been no comfortable way for him to situate himself. His restlessness had awakened her a couple of times, though she'd been careful not to let him know it. She hadn't wanted him to leave his bed on her account again. Finally he'd slept, and he was still sleeping, so when Marlys called Erin caught the phone after half a ring.

"Brenda Chase came in last night, Erin. She wants to talk to you, and I knew you'd want me to call you," Marlys said. "I could pick you up, or if you can't get away, I can try to get her to settle for Carter."

"No. I'm glad she asked for me. I'll be ready within the hour."

"How's Hunter?"

Erin glanced back over her shoulder at the man who slept in the bed she'd just left. "He had a difficult night, I think, but he's sleeping now," she said quietly, turning her back on him before she spoke. "I want to see that he makes it to the clinic again today, so I'll probably come back later."

"He won't stay down much longer, if I know Hunter," Marlys predicted.

"I know. But I intend to see that he doesn't dismiss this as a minor inconvenience and end up with an infection. I'll look for you in a little while, Marlys. Tell Brenda not to move until I get there, okay? Don't let her bolt on us again," Erin instructed. The last time she'd come to the shelter, Brenda hadn't given herself enough time. She'd gone home smiling at the first sign of contrition from her husband, and now she was back, hurting again.

Erin retrieved her clothes from the floor and drew the drapes to darken the room. The air was early-morning cool, and the room harbored the scent of the previous night's intimacy. They'd rumpled the sheets and shared the pillows. And they'd made love. She looked down at him as he slept and felt a surge of possessiveness that startled her. What she needed was a pelting shower, hot water followed by a blast of cold. Then she'd get out of there for a while and try to do some straight thinking.

Showered and dressed, she lacked only the sandals she'd left in the bedroom. She slipped in quietly, found the sandals and was about to slip out.

"Erin."

She turned toward the low rumble that had shaped her name. She hadn't heard him move, but he was braced on his elbows, the sheet tossed over his hips. In the dim light, surrounded by wood and shades of brown, he reminded her of a wounded wolf peering from his den. His eyes riveted her where she stood.

"I thought you were sleeping," she said, not knowing what else to say.

"Would you drop the articles off with Bernie and tell her I'll be in later?"

"Of course. Don't you think you should—"

"I've got work to do, and so do you. I'll get over to the clinic on my own. Believe it or not, the idea of infection doesn't appeal to me, either."

So he'd been awake. "I thought you'd probably sleep for a while, but I can make your breakfast now if you'd like."

"I'll take care of that, too, when I'm ready. What I'd like is for you to go back to the mission and take care of Brenda."

"You weren't supposed to hear that," she bristled. "That's privileged."

He hadn't intended to make her feel rebuffed. He hadn't counted on the injured look in her eyes, or the niggling satisfaction that planted in him. But he hadn't counted on needing her this morning, either, not like this. He wanted some time to get back in control. Wanting Erin was a fact of his life, but needing her was a damned poor idea.

As he lay back against the pillow Hunter closed his eyes. "The other thing I wouldn't like right now is to have you and Marlys fussing around in my kitchen. In fact, when she comes, I'd appreciate it if you wouldn't even let her in the door. I don't feel like being examined and advised by any well-intentioned friends this morning."

"All right, then," she said quietly, "I'll leave you to lick your own wounds." And just as quietly she let herself out of the house.

Erin decided that it was up to Hunter to get in touch with her. She was a mature woman, not about to let herself get starry-eyed over what they'd shared, especially after the casual dismissal he'd given her. She'd said too much. She'd given herself away. He'd sensed the feelings that arose with her that morning, the ones she'd tried to wash away. She'd wanted to call his bed *theirs*.

She waited a week. He didn't call. He didn't even get back to her about the layouts for the catalog. When she swallowed her pride and called Brave Wolf Publishing she was told that Hunter wasn't in. He was out of town, in fact, and Bernie didn't know when to expect him back. No, he couldn't be reached by phone.

Why couldn't he be reached by phone? Erin could think of one possibility. Crimson Eagle had no electricity, no running water and no telephones. She remembered the long-distance call, the references to someone for whom Hunter couldn't understand being a target, someone who was at Crimson Eagle. Hunter was at Crimson Eagle, Erin decided, and she'd find a way to get Bernie to admit it. She'd also find a way to get in there herself. Someone she loved had been killed up there, and now someone up there was threatening Hunter, whom she also loved. *Of course* she loved him; she always had. Why else would she be on her way to McLaughlin with a crazy notion like the one that was taking shape in her head?

With the motive for her madness firmly in place and the method taking shape, she turned in at Brave Wolf Publishing's gravel driveway looking for means. She saw the van with the company's name and wolf-head logo on the side, and a light in her head glimmered, gained voltage, then glowed.

"Hunter just called me," Erin informed Bernie. She'd taken Hunter's "right-hand man" into the privacy of Hunter's partially refurbished office. It smelled of fresh paint and stale soot. "He wants me to take the van down to Crimson Eagle and bring his car back.''

''What for?'' Hunter had instructed her not to tell Erin he was at Crimson Eagle, but he'd obviously changed his mind. No one else could have told her where he was.

Erin shrugged. ''He wouldn't say. Apparently they need a large vehicle. He said to be sure it was empty, so they must need the cargo space for something.''

A frown creased Bernie's pretty forehead. ''I could have taken it down there. He left me with his dog, his house key and this week's paper. Why didn't he call me about the van?''

''I guess he just doesn't want to leave the newspaper office in anybody else's hands.'' Erin wasn't usually inclined to touch people in an effort to make a conversational point, but she made an exception. Had he wanted the van, Hunter surely would have called Bernie. That being the case, Erin needed something to carry the story across, and a hand on Bernie's arm was a convincing touch. ''This paper means more to him than anything else, and he trusts you with it. No one else. I . . . envy you that, Bernie.'' As she said it, Erin knew she'd come closer to the truth than she'd meant to, and she tasted a little unexpected bitterness.

''I think it's empty,'' Bernie told her. ''I'll get the keys, and we'll make sure.''

Actually, Erin's plan called for cargo. On her way south she stopped at a grocery store and bought several boxes full of food. Though the cargo was a ruse, she suspected it might be welcome.

There was a different man at the Crimson Eagle gate this time, a fact that Erin hoped would be in her favor. This man seemed less devoted to his sentry post than the first guard she'd encountered. In fact, Erin was sure this man had been asleep in the chrome-and-vinyl kitchen chair he'd set by the gate. He carried some unnecessary weight around the middle, and he wasn't anxious to move it from the chair to the visiting van. Erin had to go to him.

"Hunter Brave Wolf asked me to bring the van up and take his car home for him," Erin announced, peering down through dark glasses. "The stuff he asked for is in the back."

"What kind of stuff?" the man asked, checking out the logo on the side of the white panel van.

"Supplies, mostly food," she answered with a sweeping gesture toward the van. "See for yourself."

The man hauled himself out of the chair and padded over to the van's back doors, his moccasined feet kicking up little puffs of dust. Erin followed, opened the doors and waited while he gave her cargo a cursory once-over. "Take it on through," he said, and he walked back over to the gate and swung it open.

The camp at the top of the dirt road struck her as both bleak and brave. There was a collection of temporary-looking buildings made of untreated wood, which had grayed from exposure. The canvas tipis and the army tents somehow looked more at home here. Several squaw coolers sheltered small groups of people, who looked up from whatever they were doing to follow the van as it rolled timidly into camp. The driver's nerve was faltering.

A young boy ducked into a tipi, and Hunter soon ducked out. Erin stood her ground beside the van, her mind buzzing with opening lines, some flippant, some humble, but none that sounded convincing anymore, not even to her. He strode toward her, his face betraying no emotion. A second man emerged from the tipi, and a third curious head popped out behind him.

Hunter said nothing until his face was inches from hers, and then his demand was ground out quietly between his teeth. "Erin, what the hell are you doing here?"

"I brought . . . supplies."

"You what?"

The two men were hanging back, and a quick glance past Hunter's shoulder told Erin that they were suspicious. She took Hunter's hand and urged, "Come on, I'll show you."

There was a little privacy between the open doors at the back of the van. Hunter surveyed the boxes quickly, then swung his gaze back to Erin. "What's this all about?"

"I had to come, Hunter."

"What'd you do, steal the van? Bernie wouldn't just let you . . . I *told* her not to tell you I was here."

"She didn't. I tricked her into letting me take the van. It was the only thing I could think of that might get me in here."

He grabbed her shoulders with both hands. "Why?"

"He's here, isn't he?" she whispered. "The man who—"

His hard kiss rocked her back on her heels and effectively shut her up. It was a fierce kiss, a warning, and when he drew back from her, his eyes narrowed on hers, restating the warning. The two men stood not more than a few feet away.

Hunter's quick smile took Erin by surprise. "That's all I really wanted," he told her. "But I thought my friends could use a change from grease bread and chopped meat. I hope you brought eggs."

She knew he'd seen the case of eggs she'd brought, and she nodded.

"We don't need any *waśicu* up here, Hunter," one of the men put in. "Especially not female. They're guaranteed trouble."

"This one's Hunter's trouble," said a third voice at Erin's back. "He'll take care of her."

Erin turned, smiled and reached for Johnny Parker's handshake. To his surprise, she wasn't satisfied with that, and she gave him what turned out to be an awkward embrace.

Hunter chuckled inwardly at Johnny's discomfort. Indians greeted one another with an easy handshake, but women reserved this kind of display for their own men in the privacy of their own homes. Erin's behavior was excusable only because she was a white woman and didn't know any better.

"Johnny, it's so good to see you," she was saying. "You haven't changed a bit. In fact," she considered, taking stock of the wiry body that was about her height, "I think you've even lost a few pounds. And you're grayed a little. Too soon, Johnny, much too soon."

"He needs a vacation," Hunter put in.

"When the president invites me to Camp David for a summit," Johnny promised. "Hunter told me you were working at the mission again."

"She shouldn't be up here," one of the other men persisted, but the complaint lacked insistence now that he'd seen that Johnny Parker knew her, too.

"I sent for her, Tim. She's my woman, and she'll be with me until I send her back." Hunter hooked an arm over Erin's shoulders and pulled her to his side.

"Take my tipi," Johnny offered, and then he grinned. "It's just like old times."

Hunter cocked his head toward the van. "Do what you want with this stuff, Johnny. We're going for a walk."

Still grinning, Johnny nodded. "Just like old times."

Hunter kept an arm firmly fastened around Erin's shoulders, saying very little as he walked her out of camp, beyond a copse of scruffy pines and up to a barren knoll. Settling his hands on her shoulders, he turned her to him. "You don't say anything down there you don't want overheard," he warned her. He looked from her face to the trees and back again. "As far as any watchers are concerned, this is strictly a conjugal visit, right? Short and sweet."

"That madman is up here, isn't he?"

"Erin, this was a foolish stunt. I want to cuss you out, but I don't think I can do it with a smile on my face. And besides," he said, pulling her to him, "our audience expects something more dramatic." His kiss was beyond the realm of drama. She clung to him and kissed him back, hoping he understood now. She counted on making him forget the tricks she'd pulled to get here. The kiss made demands, and drawing apart from it proved difficult.

"Are we really being watched?" Erin asked quietly when he looked down at her again.

"Probably."

"Why?"

"Because we're not trusted. So forget the detective bit, if that's what you came up here for. It's too dangerous. We're going to take Johnny up on his offer for a couple of hours, just so nobody thinks you're here to mess with anything but me, and then you're taking that van right back where you got it."

"I'll go when you do," she told him.

Something in the way she looked at him made him save the sarcasm. Something in the way she tightened her arms around his neck made his heart thud just a little harder. He covered her back with the palms of his hands. "I'm not staying much longer," he promised. "This is no place for you, Erin."

"I want to be where you are." Her eyes were wide with determination. "I'm afraid for you, Hunter. No one told me where you were. I knew. I felt it, and I had to come."

"I'll be all right as long as no one gets edgy, and you could make them edgy."

"Who?" she demanded.

"Anybody. Me, for starters." He rolled his eyes toward the sky and heaved a sigh. "These people are not playing games, Erin. This isn't an adventure for restless college girls. Johnny isn't a happy-go-lucky kid anymore, and I'm not . . ." The tears he saw gathering in her eyes softened him. "I don't want you to get hurt."

She blinked quickly. The tears would be a weakness, and all she wanted him to see now was strength.

"This is where they killed Louise," she reminded him, managing an even tone. "I love you, Hunter, and I'm afraid someone might shoot you in the back. I just couldn't sit by waiting to hear it on the six o'clock news."

Garbled as it was, the declaration rang in Hunter's head like the clanging of a mission bell. A one-sided smile got away from him. "You love me, and you think someone might shoot me in the back? Not a very promising future for us, Erin."

"Hunter, please. I'm not kidding."

"I was hoping you were—at least the part about my getting shot in the back."

She bit her bottom lip, waiting.

He pulled her to his chest, tightening his embrace. "How do you feel about sharing a tipi in the middle of a camp full of renegade Sioux?" he asked.

## Chapter 9

The sun drew down behind them as Hunter and Erin walked back to the camp. His arm around her shoulders left no doubt that she belonged with him. He'd get his pictures of the man he and Sam Whiteman suspected of being part of the Pan-Indian Liberators outfit and get her out of here tomorrow. Rick Morales had wedged himself in tight with Johnny, and it wasn't going to be easy to shake him loose. With Erin around, he'd have to give up on the idea of flushing Morales out this time. He squeezed the shoulder under his hand, thinking he wasn't going to let her out of his sight until they'd very casually made their way past the gate.

"How are your arms?" Erin asked, noting the healthy squeeze he'd just given her. He was wearing faded jeans and a long-sleeved Western shirt, which covered his injuries.

"Healing nicely," he replied. "I know because they itch like hell."

"Bernie's got the office all cleaned up and painted," Erin said brightly, though brightly was hardly the way she viewed Bernie's efficiency. "She didn't understand why you'd call and ask me to bring the van down instead of her."

"Why I'd ca—"

"Of course, I reminded her that she couldn't be spared," Erin cut in quickly. "That you'd trust no one else with that precious newspaper of yours."

"You must have been in fine form," Hunter mumbled.

Erin tilted him a saucy grin. "Oh, I was."

"We'll see how your form is after a night of sleeping on the ground. You just might have outsmarted yourself, Erin O'Neill."

There was a supper of frybread and soup served cafeteria-style under the rustling willow shelter of a squaw cooler. Afterward the years seemed to drop away from Johnny Parker's lean face as he sat with Hunter and Erin near a stone-rimmed fire pit just outside Johnny's tipi, which was set apart from the others as befitted his position of leadership. The three grew dreamy-eyed as they pitched twigs into the flames and recounted old times. When the camp showed signs of putting itself to bed, Johnny discreetly excused himself, leaving Hunter and Erin the privacy of his tipi.

While Hunter extinguished the fire, Erin eyed the towering fan of lodgepoles that extended above the canvas cover and pointed stiffly at the stars. Red-gold sparks skittered by, sailing among the poles and beyond into the inky night. They'd been reminiscing about campfires gone by, the ones the trio of friends had shared in the evenings when they'd gone riding together. But camping out like this was a first for Erin, and she'd never considered the inconvenience that went along with it. Use of the outdoor "facility" was the only exception Hunter allowed in his insistence that she not be out of his sight for a moment, and even then he was close by. Water for washing had to be heated, and if she wanted a bath, she was told she'd have to use the creek.

"We'll have a small fire inside," Hunter said, pulling her attention to the darkened fire pit, where, down on one knee, he was making sure the fire was cold. "It'll seem a little smoky, but it'll keep the mosquitoes away." He looked up and smiled, and she remembered why the inconveniences didn't matter. She was with Hunter, and she could see for herself that he was all right. Moreover, she was convinced, though she knew it made no sense, that as long as she was with him he couldn't be harmed.

She'd thought it would seem stuffy inside once they laced the door flap shut, but the tipi was actually two thicknesses of canvas. The outside cover stopped more than a foot short of reaching the ground, and another five-foot width of canvas was attached inside the lodgepoles. With the door flap closed, the tipi was ventilated between the canvases. Good circulation of air would draw most of the smoke through the smokehole at the top.

It wasn't fancy, but the tipi boasted two stools, obviously hand hewn from sturdy pine, and two sleeping pallets, both made up of blankets and star quilts.

Dark animal fur peeked out from under the quilts on both beds. The small stone fire pit in the center of the tipi had a wrought-iron kettle stand and a grate. Erin noticed a skillet and a Dutch oven sitting with a blue enameled coffeepot over to one side. Settling on one of the pallets, she watched Hunter build a small fire in the fire pit. He finished it off with a sprinkling of sage, which Erin knew to be a good insect repellent.

"By tomorrow I might be ready to abandon what's left of my modesty and take that creek bath," Erin mused. "I feel a little dust covered."

"That's just healthy camp grit." Hunter took up the Dutch oven and dipped water into it from a can. "We'll go down to the creek early so we can have it all to ourselves. Nobody stirs before the dew burns off the grass. Ruins the moccasins." He smiled at her across the top of the open kettle. "I want to do all I can to help you preserve your modesty now that you've told everybody you're my woman."

"Now that *I've* told..."

"Sort of links my reputation right up with yours," he told her, the grin widening. "So try to behave yourself when you're out in public, okay?"

"Behave myself!" Erin sputtered, playing the role with the proper indignation. "To whom do you think you're talking?"

"To Hunter Brave Wolf's woman. Etiquette requires you to walk five paces behind me, never eat until I've had my fill and come when I call."

"Etiquette?" she blustered. "Whose idea of—"

"Keep your eyes respectfully lowered, and never raise your voice to me," he continued, removing the steaming Dutch oven from the fire.

"I wonder which sex came up with *those* rules."

"The same one that said you couldn't vote or own property or go out without a veil over your face, but the whole plan seems to have fallen apart lately." Leaning back on an elbow, he let his eyelids drop to half mast and cocked his chin at her. "Come over here, woman," he growled.

"Is this in reference to that third rule?"

"Actually, this is rule number one: one man's woman never sleeps in another man's blankets. Those are Johnny Parker's," he pointed out. "These are mine."

"I see." Erin considered the two pallets and then started across the tipi.

"Come around this way," he instructed, motioning in a circle. "Never walk between a person and the fire. Very bad manners."

"Sorry," she mumbled, reversing direction. "I refuse to be servile, but I don't want to be rude."

"That's my woman." He reached for her hand, grinning up at her. "Always the lady. I'll make a deal with you. I'm willing to set aside all the rules but one, as long as you agree to abide by that one."

She sat, but he moved over her quickly, laying her back on the blanket. "Which one?" she asked.

"Number one." He braced himself on one elbow, looking down at her as he traced the width of her forehead and the length of her cheek with his thumb. "You will never again sleep in another man's blankets. It's driven me crazy for twelve years, knowing you were."

"I was never happy with..." The name stuck to Erin's tongue like a stamp and was equally distasteful. She hurried past it. "It was right with you. Everything else was...all wrong. I learned the hard way."

"I'll make you happy. Whenever you come to my blankets, I'll make you happy." He kissed her mouth with gently probing lips.

"Does the rule apply to you, too?" she whispered. "Will I be the only woman to...come to your blankets?"

"You're the only woman I want, Erin." He loosed the buttons on her blouse, kissed her neck and whispered hotly against her shoulder, "The only woman I've ever wanted."

"I know I have no right to be jealous, but I guess I am."

He undressed her, kissing her as he went, worshiping her with his eyes and vowing, "In my heart, there's been no place for anyone but you. Stay with me, Erin." She was naked now, and his whisper touches had left her trembling. He rose to his knees beside her, and she followed, taking his shirtfront in both hands and pulling the snaps apart, one by one. When he sat back on his heels she scooted between his knees and slipped the shirt over his shoulders, lightly touching the four small bandages on his arms as she planted a kiss in the center of his breastbone and willed him to heal quickly.

He sucked his breath in quickly. "Oh, God, Erin, stay with me and there will never be room in my blankets for anyone else."

"I love you," she said.

You loved me once and left me, Erin, he thought. This time...

She was mesmerized by his eyes as Hunter reached for a cloth and drenched it in the kettle of water. He was the wolf whose keen senses missed nothing as he waited for the moment to be right.

This time you've left them—the people in your other world—and come to me, he thought triumphantly. This time you made the choice to put yourself within my reach.

He began washing her face with firm, even strokes. The cloth was soft and warm, and it smelled sweet.

"You're bathing me," she whispered.

"Yes."

"Mmm. It feels good. All that dust..."

"Will be gone," he promised. "Along with all that's past."

She closed her eyes and let it be true. When he was done, she took the cloth from him and bathed him, too. When she reached his belly she dispensed with the snap on his jeans, and they stood together so she could push them over his hips and continue the bath. There was great satisfaction in washing the past from his body. They had agreed that it was so, and so it was. She knelt to finish his feet, and then he pulled her to stand with him by the fire. Facing one another, they took handfuls of warm water from the pot and dribbled them over each other's heads, letting the water run down their bodies, over breasts and chest, dribbling over abdomens and thighs. Rinsing rivulets of soft rainwater left them slick and wet and trembling for each other.

He ran his hands along her shoulders and down the length of her arms, marveling at the bright beauty of her wet skin. Her face, turned up to his, was dewy, and spring-green wonder shone in her eyes. The hunger grew inside him when he realized he'd never seen her look at him quite this way before. Her face held no hint of reserve, no trace of fear, no inkling of conflict. There was only trust and love, as pure as the rainwater they'd used to cleanse each other.

Sliding his hands down to clasp hers, Hunter knew only one regret, that he could not at this moment legally call her his wife. It hit him suddenly, unexpectedly, because he hadn't given marriage any real thought in recent years. Without fully understanding why he was doing it, he took the pearl ring from Erin's finger, unclasped the gold chain she wore around her neck and tossed them both to the other pallet of blankets. Now she wore nothing but the sheen of water, and he had only a turquoise ring, the silver rubbed smooth as satin by the old uncle who had worn it before him. Hunter slid the ring from his hand and placed it on hers.

The open look on her face was still there. She questioned nothing. She accepted. Lifting her mouth to his, she gave.

He took her down with him to the pile of blankets and slid his still slick body against hers, touching and tasting the sweet satin dew that covered her. Her moist nipples became hard beads in his mouth. She groaned, then groaned again when he kissed the fluttering pulse at the base of her neck. He kissed her and touched her until her breath came in little pants, and she writhed in his arms, straining to match her midline to his. He pressed a thigh between hers and smiled when she arched against him, offering the irresistible valley between her breasts for his nuzzling. Glowing with golden firelight and burning only for him, she'd never been this beautiful.

Ever the careful hunter, he made many forays over her body, seeking all the ways to excite her. Every response drew his attention, and he played every spot he found to the pitch of perfection before moving to another. Her system turned itself over to him. Her senses opened up to him, saturating themselves with the smell of woodsmoke in his hair, the sleek texture of his skin, the sound of his breathing and the taste of his mouth. He was everywhere in her but one place, and that place desperately needed to be filled with him. She reached for him and found him hot and throbbing.

His brain pounded. *Want me, Erin. Need me. Invite me. Take me.*

Her mind spun. *I want your love, Hunter. I need your love. Give me your love, and take mine.*

"Hunter?"

"Tell me."

"Love me, Hunter. Please, please love me."

"I do. I always have."

"Then put yourself inside me, because I love you, too."

The quick flurry of sparks that rose from the tipi's smokehole probably came from a burning log as it suddenly shifted into the heart of the fire pit.

"I don't suppose anyone can see through this canvas," Erin whispered, her lips half an inch from the small brown nipple on Hunter's smooth chest.

"Not really," came the quiet rumble. "It's double thickness. Shadows, maybe."

"Shadows?"

This time the rumble was a chuckle. "Silhouettes on the shade."

"Oh, no. You don't really mean ..."

"No. The fire's too small. Anyway, when you live in a situation like this, you learn to be considerate of other people's privacy." He trailed a finger along her arm, which hugged his middle. "Most of us came from big families living in small houses. You learn how to make yourself scarce at the right time."

"What happened to your parents, Hunter? You once told me they were dead, but that was all you said."

He filled his lungs and emptied them slowly. "I was pretty young when my father died. We'd moved to L.A. with the government's Relocation Program, which some bureaucrat in Washington thought up to get Indians off the reservations. Trouble was, the people needed wind and sun and open spaces, and what they got was smog and concrete. My father died during relocation. My older brothers got into training programs and stayed out there. The rest of us eventually came home." There was a pause, and then a quick summation of the last of it. "My mother managed to see us all at least into our teens before she died, too."

"How old were you then?" Erin asked.

"I was fourteen."

"Where did you go?"

"I was pretty much at loose ends. We'd been a close family before relocation. We'd lived out in the country, had a few cows, a few horses. It wasn't much, but we were getting along. Relocation kind of busted everything up. With my mother gone the mission saw me through school, but I spent a lot of time in the headmaster's office. I was hell on wheels as a teenager."

"And even into your twenties," she reminded him. "You fascinated me and frightened me at the same time with your recklessness. God, you were confusing!"

"Confusing?" He laughed. "Hell, I was just a simple cowboy."

"There was nothing simple about you," she assured him, "and I loved the very things about you that scared me. Your spirit was exciting, but too free to be contained by responsibility. Your only ambition seemed to be to take each day as it came and run with it until sunset."

"Freedom was a physical thing for me then. I had to feel the wind in my face and try out every horse anybody said couldn't be ridden. And I wanted what I wasn't supposed to have." He paused, measuring the width of her delicate wrist with his fingers, and then quietly added, "You, for instance."

"Is that why you wanted me?"

"I wanted you from the first because you were beautiful, but I found other reasons as we got to know each other. Underlying it all, I think, was the unspoken dare: take her, she's not supposed to be yours." It was the first time he'd admitted that to himself, and he realized the freedom to admit it came with the fact that it didn't count anymore. "But then I found myself in love with you, and damned if that didn't complicate everything."

"I know," she said. It was true. He'd been attractive because he was dangerous and forbidden, but she'd learned to love him because he was Hunter.

"The first time you made love to me," she began, remembering how it had happened, how desperate they'd become after backing away so many times, "did you love me then?"

She had to wait several moments for his answer. "I guess I thought it would bind you to me, and that scared the hell out of me at first. But then, yes, I loved you—as much as I was capable of loving anyone at the time. I wanted you to be mine. You taught me a lesson about loving . . . and about freedom."

She swallowed hard. It was all behind them now, but she wanted to know everything he'd felt then. "What lesson?"

"When you didn't come back I thought of going out there to get you." He chuckled. "I could just see it. One kiss and you weren't going to be able to tell me you didn't love me. But the idea of you coming back on your own held more appeal, so I waited. I tried running again, but I couldn't find the same satisfaction I'd once found in pure wildness. Physical freedom wasn't enough anymore. I intellectualized the need to be free. It became a need to do what I was meant to do and do it well. And always, in the back of my mind, you were there. You were an irritant—an itch I couldn't quite scratch."

"I guess that's better than being the witch you couldn't quite catch, or worse." He laughed, but she didn't. "Oh, God, Hunter, it was awful thinking how you must have hated me. I was legally committed to one man while I belonged to another, and it was no one's fault but my own. But the worst was thinking how you must have hated—"

"Shh." He curled his arm tighter around her shoulders and laced his fingers in her hair. "We washed all that away. I never hated you, Erin. Never. There were times when I wanted to shake you till your teeth rattled, but there was never a time when I hated you." He continued stroking her hair back from her temple. "Irritants can be good, you know. Oysters make pearls because of them."

"And what did you make because of me?"

"A damned good newspaper man. Maybe too good. If you'd irritated me just long enough to make me mediocre, I might not be so idealistic about..." Groaning, he shifted to his side and braced himself on an elbow. "I don't want to get started on that. Just you and me. That's all I want to talk about." Her eyes lit up, and he smiled. "Do you really remember the first time we made love?" She nodded. "I was awful, wasn't I?"

"What do you mean, *you* were awful? Did you think it was your show?"

He raised a brow in surprise and then chuckled. "Yeah, in those days I guess I did. When you said yes, I immediately started shaking all over, and all I could think of was how was I going to take care of all those buttons and zippers without letting you see my hands shake."

"As I remember," she began, returning the smile, "nothing came off completely." Their eyes shared a dance to the tune of a memory that was theirs only. He touched her cheek, and she turned a kiss into his palm. "I felt your hands tremble, and I thought it was beautiful."

"Did you love me then, that first time?" he asked.

"I can't remember not loving you, Hunter," she whispered. "Even when I was afraid, as I was that first time."

"But not this time," he murmured.

"This time I'm not afraid to meet you halfway and make it *our* show." Her hand slowly made its way down the front of his torso. She glanced up and watched his eyes become dark embers as she touched him. "Teach me to please you," she implored in a whiskey voice.

"Teach...Erin!" Her name was drawn in on a quick breath. She froze for a moment, then experimented with a soft caress, which evoked a guttural groan. "You seem to have a gift for pleasing me. Don't...stop."

There was no stopping, nothing held back. He gave himself freely, seeking only to love her. She took him into herself and loved him fully in return. Every touch was a gift, each sigh a thanksgiving, and therein the bond was made.

Just before daybreak Erin and Hunter walked upstream from the camp to a spot secluded by a grove of trees. There they bathed, dried each other and dressed quickly. Cuddling together in a blanket, they watched a new day unfold in a red Dakota dawn.

Crimson Eagle Camp was run as a commune, with a loosely structured democratic government that gave everyone a voice as well as a duty. It seemed to work fairly well. Food and accommodations were shared, jobs were done by assigned groups and the forty-one members seemed content. Typically nothing was hurried, but everything got done in good time. The grounds were kept clean, the supply of firewood was ample, and there was plenty of time for activities. Erin noticed many of the same crafts in the making as those in the works at the mission. Small group discussions, however, seemed to be the most popular pastime.

Hunter was allowed to take his pictures of the camp, but he was warned against photographing camp members without their permission. "People get pretty touchy about that," Johnny Parker explained. He'd joined Hunter and Erin as they strolled about the campgrounds. "We don't ask them why they're here. They're entitled to their privacy. Of course, the FBI has us all on file, and we'll live with that the rest of our lives." He turned a friendly grin on Hunter. "But, hell, old friend, you can have all the pictures you want of me. Run 'em in the *New York Times* if you can. We haven't been in the news much lately."

"Is that what this is all about, Johnny? Publicity?" Erin knew the answer, but she wondered how Johnny would describe his efforts.

"Pretty much," he said, shrugging one lean shoulder. "This particular piece of federal land is land that should be ours."

"It's about treaty rights, then?"

It was a question Johnny had to answer for himself every time he got up in the morning. He often found himself wondering what the hell he was doing there. The three had reached a shallow grove of pines at the camp's edge. A fallen tree seemed as good a place as any to stop, turn and survey the little community from a distance. Johnny had been out there more than a year now. The first summer it had been like a game. There were strategy sessions and pep talks, and they'd

all found organized defiance to be a heady thing. Pre-
dictions were that, come the first snowfall, the band
of rebels would pack up and go home. No strangers to
hard times, they'd stayed.

Johnny toed the fallen log with his boot, then
turned his attention back to Erin. "It's about being
invisible."

Feeling the eyes of both men on her, Erin suddenly
felt very much an outsider. Her pale skin burned, and
she glanced away. She had no idea how it felt to be invisible.

"I'm sorry about what happened to your sister,"
Johnny offered after a brief silence. "I want you to
know she had no enemies here. Neither have you."

Erin accepted Johnny's concern with a nod. She
understood the status she'd been granted. She wasn't
the representative of a whole race of people. She was
just Erin O'Neill.

"Where did it happen exactly?" Erin asked. She
saw the look Johnny flashed Hunter over the top of
her head, and she cleared her throat to steady her
voice. "Where was Louise killed?"

"She was between the women's privy and the
creek," Johnny told her. "The shot was fired from
across the creek."

"Why haven't the police found out who did it?"

Johnny's small, black eyes narrowed as he swung
his gaze back in the direction of the camp. "I don't
think they want to. I think they wanted to prove it was
one of us, and when that didn't pan out, they stopped
looking."

Erin turned to Hunter. "Do you think that's possible?"

"Anything's possible," Hunter said, and then he shot a glance at Johnny. "But that theory is improbable, and Johnny knows it."

"Politics is behind everything that happens to us," Johnny returned. "You know damned well we've been a political football ever since we put the skids to Custer's plans to redecorate the White House."

"That's true," Hunter said, squatting to make use of the log as a seat. "Which is why the FBI would have preferred to have Louise's murder cleared up and forgotten as quickly as possible." He waited while Erin sat beside him and Johnny took the space next to her. "It wouldn't take much to move you out of here, John. You know that."

"We'd fight," Johnny insisted, snapping a dry twig between his fingers.

"You'd lose. They'd clear you out today except they don't want to risk any bad press." Forearms draped over his knees, Hunter drummed home his point with the side of one hand against the palm of the other. "Because the federal government has such a wonderful history of bungling Indian affairs, we have an edge with the press. Public sympathy is generally on our side. Washington doesn't want any incidents up here. As long as it's nice and quiet now, my guess is they'll let you guys occupy this rock forever."

"What about Alcatraz?" Erin put in, recalling the activists' takeover of the abandoned federal penitentiary. "They put a stop to that."

"Alcatraz was *visible*," Hunter reminded her. "People were pumping a lot of dimes into those waterfront binoculars. What we have here," he said, an open-handed gesture indicating the camp, "is a miniature reservation. Nice out-of-the-way spot. Who's to notice a few renegade Indians up here?''

"So what are you saying, Hunter?" Johnny challenged. "You think we should just give up?"

"I'm saying you've made your point. Incidents like Louise's murder don't do the cause any good. Neither does firebombing my office."

Neither man looked at the other, but Erin felt Johnny's whole body stiffen as the three sat side by side, ostensibly viewing the little camp.

"Are you saying you think those incidents came from within the movement?" Johnny's voice was quiet and steely.

"I'm beginning to wonder how many movements are at work here, John," Hunter answered. "What do you really know about Rick Morales?"

"I know I can trust him." The answer came quickly, as though in response to a threat.

"Since when don't you trust me?" Hunter asked quietly.

Johnny laced his fingers together and let his arms droop over his knees. He was tired, and his slow sigh was a dead giveaway. Leadership of the group had not been his own choice, and Hunter knew that well. "I followed Ray Two Bows in this. I never thought he'd get himself arrested and leave me standing out there in front. I could've used your help, Hunter."

"This isn't my way. I do what I can for you at the typewriter, but I'm not going to be much good to anybody if these attacks on my office keep up. Somebody's obviously looking to stir up a hornet's nest, and he's decided that going after Brave Wolf Publishing is the way to do it."

Johnny reached down for another twig. "Morales has been with me since Ray was arrested. I've always been able to count on him to help me sort things out. Being from New Mexico, he brings in an unbiased viewpoint. He's got no relatives to please here."

"I think his relatives can be found quite a ways south of New Mexico," Hunter suggested.

"What do you mean?"

"I think he may be with the Pan-Indian Liberators."

The twig in Johnny's hand snapped as he swung his head in Hunter's direction. "They're terrorists," he protested. "Rick's no terrorist. This action was never intended to be anything but a peaceful demonstration."

"The Pan-Indian Liberators were behind some trouble out in L.A. They like to turn peaceful demonstrations like yours into violent confrontations," Hunter explained. "They have this idea that Indians from Chile to Alaska should unite and take what's coming to them, so the plan is to stir up the discontented. I think Morales is here to heat things up."

"Why would a terrorist go after you?" Johnny questioned.

"Or Louise," Erin added. "She only wanted to help."

Hunter knew he was only theorizing, and he didn't like to vocalize too many theories without proof. "Louise was with the church, and several of the churches have pulled back from us since she was killed." He sighed, flexing his shoulders, and continued to outline his suspicions. "I represent a free, independent Indian press. My job is to keep people informed, see that they have enough information to make judgments. That's not good for business if you're a terrorist. You do better with ignorance and half-truths if you want people to go off half-cocked and set the reservation on fire.''

Johnny studied the broken twig, scraping the thin bark with his thumbnail. Years ago he would have followed Hunter into the fires of hell if only Hunter had given the word. But Hunter wasn't with him now, and Rick Morales was. Johnny wasn't a decision maker. He needed Morales. ''You're wrong this time, Hunter,'' Johnny said finally. ''Morales is no terrorist.''

Slowly Hunter got to his feet. Stepping behind the log, he laid a hand on his friend's shoulder. ''Do yourself a favor, John. Be a little suspicious. You've got good judgment. Trust it.'' Without looking up, Johnny nodded. ''*Use* it,'' Hunter insisted. Johnny sighed and nodded again.

When they were alone again Erin turned to Hunter with a sad-eyed request. ''Show me where it happened. I want to see exactly where she died.''

It would not have been his choice to show her such a place, where tradition warned that an uneasy spirit might reside. He dismissed the superstition that to mention a dead person's name was to court disaster, but a belief in ghosts was too deeply rooted in his heritage to be totally ignored. Nevertheless, the look in Erin's eyes told him that this was important to her. Wordlessly he slipped an arm around her shoulders and walked her to a place near the bank of the gently flowing creek.

Without any indication from Hunter, Erin's eyes found the patch of ground she'd asked to see. She glanced across the creek, then back at the grassy spot. For a moment she forgot Hunter's presence as she felt Louise's. A gentle breeze carrying the clean scent of pine stung Erin's eyes. When she turned Hunter was there, quietly waiting. She went to him, and he held her while she wept.

## Chapter 10

Erin wondered if the evening fare ever varied at Crimson Eagle. The soup was hearty, the frybread filling, and no one at the communal supper mentioned that it was a repeat of the previous night's meal. It could have used a little salt and pepper, she thought as she spooned the last bit of corn and beef broth from the bottom of the blue enamelware bowl. The dishes and utensils were Hunter's. Erin had forgotten the only requirements for an Indian "feed": bring your own dishes and eat your fill.

It was twilight, and a breeze whisked through the treetops at the camp's back. Hunter had finished his meal and was reclining on an elbow next to Erin, nursing a cup of black coffee. Erin declined the coffee. *Wakalyapi* was the Lakota word for it, and it had a life of its own. Coffee grounds were boiled over the fire, and then cold water was added. The brew was lukewarm, and strong enough to dissolve rust.

Hunter turned a warm smile her way when Erin put her empty bowl in his and slid them both to the edge of the blanket they shared near the crackling campfire. His gift of a simple smile caused a rush of good feelings to tingle inside her. The sharing between them was becoming a natural and comfortable thing. Here in this camp, where day-to-day living was stark in its simplicity, pure joy and pure pain were unclouded by unnecessary trappings. With complications set aside, this time with Hunter felt good.

"They're rolling out the drum," Hunter observed, lazily stretching his long back as he sat up. A jerk of his chin indicated a big bass drum that was being set up near a squaw cooler. "Feel like dancing?"

"Are you a dancer?" Erin wondered. She hugged her knees and let the breeze blow her hair back from her face.

"'Fraid not," he admitted, shrugging. "I'm a mission school Indian. When I was growing up parents only 'talked Indian' when they didn't want us to understand the conversation, and teachers figured we'd do better in the long run if we learned to square dance rather than Indian dance. Traditional dancing is back in style now, with some new variations. It's become highly competitive and very expensive. You have to have extravagant costumes to go after the big prize money." He raised one cynical brow as he watched the drummers gather—five of them, each with his own sheepskin-wrapped drum beater. "I guess that's one way to revive dying traditions. Give them some status—make them worth money."

"Things must've changed," Erin said. "I don't remember many elaborate costumes when I was here before."

"You won't see many tonight, either. These people left all that behind. This is what you call 'back to the basics.'"

The serving table was being cleared off, though the frybread would stay there until it was gone. A couple of men squatted by the fire over another helping of soup, and a young couple across the way shared a kiss in the dark shadows. The basics were easy and comfortable.

"Have you ever felt inclined to become part of this?" Erin wondered.

Hunter shook his head slowly. "Only to observe and report. Those are my basics. In the last century I'd have been the *eyapaha*, the guy who walked around camp announcing the news."

That image played across Erin's mind, and she giggled. "I always pictured this fierce warrior called Hunter Brave Wolf—"

"Or Brave Wolf Hunter, which was my great-grandfather's name."

"Brave Wolf Hunter, then, all painted and feathered, dashing across the plains on a flashy paint."

"With you hanging over the horse's withers and screaming for help." She shrugged off the knowing glance he gave her, and he reached over to tuck a piece of yellow hair behind her ear. "You know why we have such trouble figuring out who the hell we are?" She shook her head. "Because of all the Hollywood hoopla and paperback book covers like what you just described. I actually had this mental picture of myself riding that very pony right up onto your white-columned porch out there in Connecticut. My blood-curdling war whoop would've struck terror in the heart of the guy barbecuing in his backyard next door.''

"How exciting! One kiss and I could never have denied my love for you." Her green eyes danced at the thought.

"I don't know if kissing was part of the culture, to tell you the truth." The idea was dismissed with a shrug. "Anyway, I couldn't have pulled it off unless I'd gotten roaring drunk first. So you see the problem. The images are impossible to live with. They're either ridiculous—" the alternative came harder "—or pathetic."

"You don't drink anymore, do you." It was a conclusion rather than a question.

The shake of his head needed no accompanying explanation. "They don't allow it up here, either, which is part of the decision these people have made in coming here." The look in his eyes hinted at an inner strength. "We're learning."

The drummers had begun to pound out a heart-beat, all striking in unison. Only one man wore his gray hair in traditional braids. The others, varying degrees of younger, wore a variety of lengths of straight hair, some bound across the forehead with bandannas. People were gathering around as the drummers' voices blended into one sound, a high-pitched croon that seemed to talk to the wind. No one wore the much-touted feathered or fringed costumes, but, one by one, several young people peeled away from the group to launch the dance.

Most of the women stood to the side, bouncing rhythmically at the knees, but a few joined the men in a whirling, shuffling, toe-stomp-toe-stomp step. The dancing wasn't an exhibit; it was a physical expression of the heartbeat's universal rhythm.

Absorbed in the drumbeat, Erin hadn't noticed the strange man's approach, but Hunter knew they'd been under his scrutiny all evening. He'd known the minute the dark figure moved out of the shadows, and he stiffened, waiting. The figure came toward them slowly and squatted down at the edge of their blanket.

Firelight flooded the long, thin face, but there was no light in the man's coal-dark eyes. Without a word he extended a pack of cigarettes, one filter protruding above the rest. Hunter hesitated a moment before drawing the cigarette out, then placed it between his lips and eyed the man, who snapped a match into flame with a thumbnail.

Erin watched the strange proceedings in silence, wondering whether she'd be offered a cigarette, too. Hunter stretched his chin toward the flame, drew on the cigarette, then aimed a stream of smoke just to the left of the man's ear. When the man pocketed the pack Erin decided that whatever this ritual was, it did not include her.

"Parker calls you his friend." The voice was deep and hollow, and the slight accent could easily have suggested one of the southwestern tribes. "I read your newspaper, and I don't think I agree."

"Parker calls you his friend, too, but since I don't know you, I have no opinion."

"My name is Morales." The accent seemed more pronounced on the name. "And I think you have an opinion about everything, Mr. Newspaperman. Even things you know nothing about."

Hunter studied the cigarette in his hand as he let another lungful of smoke drift from his mouth. It would take days for the nicotine to clear his system, but sharing a smoke was part of the process of sizing each other up. "Enlighten me, Morales." Black eyes met black eyes. "Where are you from?"

"New Mexico."

"Near the border?" The man nodded, and Hunter stretched one leg out, draping an arm over his upraised knee. "Probably out in the sticks someplace, right? Nobody I know down there would know you."

"Morales is a common name," the man replied with a shrug.

"Ever been in L.A.?" Morales returned a noncommittal stare. "Your face is familiar," Hunter said. "Thought I might've run into you before."

"I've been told I'm not a man most people enjoy running into. If we'd met, I think you would remember."

Hunter took a long, slow drag on his cigarette, stretching out the uncomfortable silence. Thoughtfully watching his smoke dissipate in the night air, he seemed completely at ease, while Erin's stomach had knotted itself into painful tightness.

For a moment Hunter considered the burning cigarette. "What do you think of our American cigarettes, Morales?"

"They're available in New Mexico. Even out in the sticks, near the border." The man uncoiled himself and walked away, back into the shadows.

Leaning forward, Hunter flicked the rest of the cigarette into the fire. Erin watched him study the flames, and she realized that her heartbeat had tagged itself to the drum, which had steadily picked up its pace. She waited for a comment, but none was forthcoming. Hunter's face had become solid rock. Sometime later he suggested they return to the tipi.

"Hunter!" The couple turned to find Johnny Parker following close behind them. "I need to talk with you," he explained. "Let's go inside."

A kerosene lantern threw large, eerie shadows on the tipi walls as the three sat close enough together to be able to talk quietly. "What's on your mind, John?" Hunter asked. Since the confrontation with Morales, his voice had hardened, too.

"I had a talk with Rick this evening, and I'm convinced he's not the man you think he is."

There was no mistaking the disgust in Hunter's half smile. "What did you do, John? Did you ask him if he's a terrorist? When he denied it, did you make him say, 'Honest Injun'?" Johnny scowled at Hunter, denying nothing. "Hell, John, I didn't think I had to ask you to keep what I told you to yourself."

"You made some serious accusations against a man I've come to rely on," Johnny returned. "I had to find out whether they were true."

"Asking him point-blank was not the way." Hunter sighed. There was no point in trying to tell Johnny what he had seen in Morales tonight—what the words

Morales said had told him. "Does Morales have any close followers in camp here?" he asked finally.

"We have committees. Morales is head of the Camp Welfare Committee, and there are two other men who work very closely with him. They've come to regard him as highly as I do."

"And what is the purpose of this welfare committee?" Hunter asked.

"To see to the well-being and the security of the camp. We must look out for ourselves, Hunter. We are resented even by many of our own people, who don't understand what we're trying to do here."

"Listen, my friend, if you believe everything Morales says, he'll soon have you thinking I'm a capitalist pig and Erin's with the CIA. His kind deals heavily in paranoia." Hunter glanced at Erin, adding, "Which is why we're getting out of here tonight."

"It's a long drive, and there isn't much between here and the mission," Johnny reminded him, "but suit yourselves. Before you go, though, I'll have to ask you for all of the film you shot while you were here."

Hunter eyed Johnny dispassionately for just a moment before turning to his camera bag. In another moment he handed Johnny a handful of film cans.

"The one in the camera, too," Johnny said quietly, and Hunter complied. "I'll see that you get most of them back," Johnny promised.

"Except anything there might be of Rick Morales," Hunter assumed as he repacked his equipment.

"Or anyone else who preferred not to be photographed. But the rest—they go to the *New York*

*Times*." As he filled his denim jacket pocket with film cans, Johnny ventured a smile at his old friend.

It was a sad fact that Johnny Parker simply was not the man for this job, Hunter thought. He was a follower, not a leader. "I want you to be careful, John."

"You're wrong about Morales."

"Maybe. But you need to be a little more cautious, just the same."

"Who's getting after who about being paranoid?" With a friendly slap on the back Johnny discounted all that Hunter had said. "You're the one who should be careful. It's been months since anybody's even slashed a tire on me. You're getting all the action, and I'm beginning to feel left out."

With Johnny's help Hunter loaded his belongings into his car and left quietly, leading the way, while Erin followed in the van.

At night the two-lane prairie highway was unbounded. Milestones of civilization were few and far between, and the headlights of oncoming cars appeared so infrequently that Erin found herself squinting and turning away until they whizzed past. The two red taillights up ahead were her assurance that she was not alone, but periodically they would slip out of sight, and then she felt the night all around her. She saw herself as a low-flying bird, or a bat, whose great black wings were the flatlands stretching on either side of her as she skimmed along her course.

Erin had switched off the radio when all bands went from drifting signals to static. The droning motor had been some comfort at first, but by now it had become more monotonous than silence. She'd lost track of time and of any sense of the distance she had traveled. A curve swung to the right, and two glassy eyes stared into her headlights. Erin automatically ducked her head as a sudden flutter of gray and white cleared the windshield and passed unscathed above the van. An owl. The identification came as an afterthought.

Hunter's car had disappeared over a hill, but there were bright lights behind her. Erin wished the driver would turn off his high beams as he drew closer. Angrily swiveling the too-bright rearview mirror toward the ceiling, she slowed down as an invitation for the car to pass. Now the side mirror glared at her, and Erin glanced away, expecting the car to swish past. Instead, the brightness intensified, and a sudden jolt had her fighting for control of the van.

One good nudge and Erin knew the empty van would fishtail. It was too top-heavy for this kind of game; she'd end up rolling. As she hit the lock button with her elbow she formed a mental plan. Hunter, her brain shouted, turn around! She pulled over, slipped the transmission into Park and, flicking the release on her seat belt, reached across the passenger seat to slam down the lock on the other door.

Erin ducked behind the driver's seat. Her hand struck the end of something hard, and she pulled a tire iron from beneath the seat, clutching it in both hands. The car had pulled over with her, its lights still fixed in the van's side mirror. One door slammed, then another, and Erin swallowed hard to force her pounding heart back down her throat. Wham! Something hit the side of the van. Ka-bam! Ka-bam! Ka-bam! It was an ugly, metallic version of the rhythm of the drum.

"Brave Wolf! Stay away from Crimson Eagle! Stay away from Johnny Parker!" Ka-bam!

The van rocked. She should have stayed in the seat, Erin thought wildly. She should have stayed buckled in the seat. She hadn't noticed the terrain beyond the shoulder of the road, and she had a fleeting vision of going down a hill inside a rolling van. But the rocking stopped, and there was a moment's peace. Car doors slammed again, tires squealed and the car retreated in the direction from which it had come.

Erin waited. Another car pulled up; another car door opened. It had to be Hunter. She gripped the tire iron and gritted her teeth. *Please be Hunter.*

He rapped on the side window! "Erin! Erin, are you in there? Oh, my God, what . . ."

Erin scrambled around the seat, but he was gone. Then she heard a key clicking in the back door, and she hurled herself in that direction.

"Erin, are you . . ." The dark interior of the van brightened as the light clicked on and he saw Erin's face. He reached up, and she was in his arms. "Thank God! I saw the way that car pulled away, and I thought you were gone." His hold was fierce, his fingers digging into her back and gripping the back of her head, tangling in her hair. His brain reverberated with thanks.

Reason resurfacing, Hunter reached behind his back and eased an iron poker away from his shoulder blade. "What's this?"

Erin looked down at the tire iron still clutched in her fist. It took a conscious effort to relax her hand and surrender her weapon. "They ran me off the road. They were banging on the van, rocking it . . . I thought . . . I hope you brought your gun," she breathed, "even if it's only good for killing rattle-snakes."

"You don't go up to Crimson Eagle with a gun," he told her, sizing up the tire iron's potential.

"*You* don't go back to Crimson Eagle at all. That's what he said."

"What exactly..." Glancing over his shoulder at the dark road behind, Hunter reconsidered. "We've gotta get out of here." He released her, then shoved the van's back door closed, balanced the tire iron in one hand, took her arm in the other, and hustled her across the road to his car. It took him another moment to move the van off the pavement and head the car north.

"Now," Hunter said at the tail end of a long sigh, "what exactly did he say?" Erin recounted the warning word for word. "He thought I was driving, then," Hunter concluded.

"I guess so. I think I heard two doors slam, but I only heard one voice. I didn't see them, and I don't think they saw me. I'm a fast hider."

"I'd like to think he was going after me directly. Did you recognize the voice?" She shook her head, but he persisted. "Was it the man at the campfire?"

"I don't know."

Hunter wondered if Morales knew that the best way to terrorize him was to threaten Erin. He shot her a worried glance. "Erin, I want you to go home. Now. Tomorrow."

Now that she was safe, her voice held a newfound bravado. "I will not. That man was after you, not me. *You're* the one who should be skipping the territory. I was just in the wrong place at the wrong time—again."

"Listen, Erin, the man knows I'm on to him. I've either got to nail him soon or he'll be gone. He knows my weaknesses—Brave Wolf Publishing and you. I want you out of the way."

There was a long silence. It was security versus risk again. Erin still trembled inside from the scare she'd had, but she was okay. She thought of the sniper and the firebombing and the long, lean face with the deep-set dark eyes. Twelve years ago she had deliberated, considered the possibilities, listened to "reason." This time her mind scoffed at all that. There was no doubt. "I'm staying," she informed him quietly.

Hunter stopped at the next little town's gas station, which was closed but had a phone booth out front. He called the county sheriff to report the incident, admitting that he could not identify the driver, nor could he describe the car. He described the location of the van with reference to the closest highway mile markers and was promised that the sheriff would check on the vehicle.

In the early-morning hours Hunter's car pulled up in front of the girls' dorm at the mission. Shutting off the motor, he turned in his seat, one arm draped over the top of the steering wheel, and faced Erin. The yard light cast his stern face into shadow. "This would all be much easier if I only had myself to worry about."

"That is all you need to worry about, Hunter. For whatever reason, this man is trying to hurt you, not me."

His hand shot toward her suddenly and cupped her jaw. Erin caught her breath as the lamplight slanted across his face and illuminated the fear in his eyes. "The best and the worst way for him to hurt me would be through you. I want you where I know you're safe, and that, unfortunately, is not with me right now. I'm not going to see you for a while, Erin.''

"Hunter..."

"And you are *not* going to try to see me." She pressed her hand against his, and his stomach tightened. "I'm going to call Perry Trueblood and tell him what the score is. He'll watch out for you. Perry's a good cop. As long as you stick close to the mission, you'll be okay."

"What about you?"

Hunter hoped to reassure her with a grin. "I've got more on Morales than he realizes." Pulling his hand back, he produced a film can from the pocket of his denim jacket. "Johnny didn't search me, which must mean he still has some trust in me. Sam Whiteman wants this Morales as badly as I do, and Sam's a bloodhound. You just listen to me and stay put, and things'll work out just fine." He flashed her a confident wink. "I'll call you every night and whisper sexy suggestions in your ear."

"How long will it be?"

"I don't know," he said quickly. "Not long. Come on, I'll walk you to your door."

They found subtle ways to postpone his leaving. It took longer to walk to the back door than it would have to the front, and the pace was that of two people more concerned with the distance between their bodies than between departure and destination. Tucked under Hunter's arm, Erin slipped her own arm under his demin jacket and around his waist.

"Cold?" he murmured, giving her upper arm a brisk rub.

Erin shook her head, letting Hunter turn her to face him. They'd reached the bottom of the back steps, but neither made any move to mount them. Beneath his open jacket she found the way around him with both arms, tucked her face against the side of his neck and hugged him close. "I don't want you to go," she whispered.

He smiled up at the crowd of stars that watched them and tightened his hold on her. After all this time and all the growing up they'd done, it was still the same scene at the back door. He filled his lungs with damp night air. "Oh, Erin, believe me, I don't want to go. I want to crawl in bed with you and drift off to sleep making slow, lazy love. But it wouldn't look too good in the morning, would it?"

"No," she admitted, nuzzling inside his collar. "Let's just stay like this."

"I haven't got that kind of willpower. Let's take a walk out to the corral. Say hello to Gambler." Taking one of her hands from the back of his waist, he tugged her along with him. Erin laughed. The walk out to the corral was always good for an extra half an hour together.

Hunter didn't need to turn the lights on in the barn. Nothing ever changed; nothing was ever moved. Bright starlight illuminated the corral, and the smell of feed brought the horse to his master. After being treated to an extra measure of oats Gambler showed a definite lack of interest in further visiting. Hunter and Erin wandered into the hay yard, getting farther away from the mission buildings.

Square bales of hay were piled in several neat ziggurat-style stacks. Hunter remembered a time when

the mission's hay had been part of his job. He'd hated
it. The little Ford tractor only worked half the time,
and he'd preferred the saddle to a tractor seat any day.
Now one of the local farmers cut hay on the mission's
land for two-thirds of the crop, and the mission's
share, except what Hunter bought for his horses, was
sold. Hunter didn't miss putting up hay, but he did
miss walking among the stacks he'd built, counting the
layers and knowing he'd put them there, every one.

They slowed to a standstill, and Erin sat on a ledge
of bales at the front of a stack. The cut hay prickled
the backs of her legs and crackled beneath her as she
shifted to get comfortable. Balancing one booted foot
on the corner of a bale, Hunter crossed his forearms
over his knee and leaned toward her. "It's just like old
times, isn't it?" he said quietly. "It's tough to say
good-night."

The inclination to nod in agreement was cut off by
a second thought. "It isn't *just like* it used to be.
Those are sweet memories, but we're different people. We don't even love the same way we did then."
She looked up and found him studying her. "We have
more to give each other now."

He wasn't sure how much of her assessment was
true. It was true that he had more to give her now, and
he wanted to believe that she had more to give him.
But lately he'd also given her a lot of trouble. At least
when he'd been just a cowboy nobody had ever shot
at him. Times had changed in the West. These days the
bad guys were shooting at newspapermen.

"When this is all cleared up, we'll—" Hunter
straightened, tuning toward an intruding sound.
Cocking her head with a frown, Erin tried to pick up

what he heard, but he snatched her from her seat before she knew what the alarm was all about.

With Erin in tow Hunter circled the larger haystack and ducked behind a small one, pulling Erin with him into the nest of a broken bale. He pushed her head down and popped his over the low wall the bales made. In a moment he slid down beside her, his back against the wall. Erin's anxious look was met by silent laughter. Hunter held his sides to keep from bursting with it.

"What—"

"Shh!" He raised a finger to his own lips first and then to hers. A beam of light swept the ground in front of them, vanished for a moment, then skimmed over the tufts of grass and scattered bits of hay just below their feet. Erin sat still, huddled next to the haystack, and held her breath. Retreating footsteps sounded good to Erin, but they seemed to strike Hunter even funnier than before. Tilting his head back, he laughed silently at the stars.

"What's so funny?" was Erin's hushed demand.

"It's Trueblood."

"Then why are we hiding?"

"Because we don't want to get caught," he whispered, hooking an arm around her neck and silencing her with a kiss. "Do we?"

Erin smiled and shook her head. The conscientious policeman poked around a while longer. Hunter and Erin could hardly contain themselves when they heard him mumbling to himself. "Thought sure I heard voices. Damned mice, probably. Three o'clock in the morning... never get back to sleep. Damned mice sound just like people whispering."

When he was gone they let their laughter find voice as they slid down into the loose hay like two figures of melting wax. Soft and malleable, they molded readily to each other, hands smoothing one another's curves until there was no space between them, no separateness. Holding each other, they let their laughter float quietly in the night air, drifting first into one sigh, then another.

The hay was newly mown and still smelled green— a combination of late alfalfa and sweet clover. It smelled of dust and sunshine. Erin rolled over Hunter and ran a stiff straw along his jawline. It reached the corner of his mouth, and he grabbed it with his teeth and pulled it away. Chewing on the end of the straw, he eyed her pointedly. "Care for a roll in the hay, lady?"

"Ladies don't roll in the hay."

"What do they do? Frolic?"

"Or cavort."

"Rolling's more fun." He reversed their positions and hovered over her on his elbows, grinning down at her. The straw was still clamped between his white, even teeth. "See?"

"Have you ever given frolicking a try?"

"Uh-uh."

"It takes a certain finesse."

"Lady, you've got enough finesse for both of us," he judged, letting the straw tickle her chin.

"It also requires a great deal of self-control. How are you fixed for self-control, cowboy?"

"Try me."

She gave him a coy smile and took the end of the straw in her own teeth. They tugged it between them like two puppies at play until Hunter won out, turned his head to the side and blew the toy away. Then he dived in for a kiss.

Inhaling his masculine scent deeply, she drew the taste of him into her mouth as her arms burrowed beneath his jacket. His back felt hard and warm, the well-worn cotton shirt soft beneath the palms of her hands. She gave him kiss for kiss and felt his excitement rise with hers. When he ducked his head for a taste of her neck, she nibbled his ear. He groaned, and his hands found their way underneath her shirt and pullover. He counted her ribs with his fingertips as he went. She answered in kind, freeing his shirt from the confines of his jeans. Her bra went slack, and he pushed the material out of the way, his mouth seeking her breasts. Before he could turn her will to jelly, she reached down to spread a caress across the front of his jeans. He lifted his head to draw a ragged breath, and she cupped him firmly in her hand.

All breathing was suspended while Erin unfastened his belt and unzipped his jeans. He would be hers first this time. He didn't move until she had him cradled in her palm.

"Oh, God, Erin...I won't be able to..."

"I think you will, love," she whispered. "I think you always will. You have such wonderful strength, and yet here—" he drew a sharp breath "—here you're so vulnerable. You need my protection, the shelter of my body."

"Erin..."

"In the moment you lose control..."

"Sweet heaven, Erin..."

"You'll be safe inside me."

"I want to be . . . inside you. . . ."

With an unsteady hand he unsnapped her jeans and tugged at the zipper. She helped him, lifted her hips to his hand and sighed when he touched her. "Now, Erin, I can't wait."

"Now, Hunter . . . I love you—"

"Love you . . . love you, Er—rin."

Her name became the whisper of the night wind, the quiet rustle of newly mown hay, the throaty breath of stars in a deep prairie sky.

## Chapter 11

"So much for my self-control." Hunter chuckled low in his throat as he adjusted his clothes with one hand and held Erin close with the other. "You can be quite a little vixen, Erin O'Neill."

"A vixen is a fox. I don't want to be a fox." Snuggling into his jacket, she splayed her fingers over his stomach. "What do you call a lady wolf?"

"A she-wolf."

"A she-wolf! Isn't there a more poetic term?"

"I doubt it. Wolves aren't as cute as foxes. They've tended to get pretty bad press." He laughed when he heard what he'd said. "Had to start our own press to change our image."

"Well, if you'd stop running around dressed like sheep, and stop scaring little girls in the woods..."

His sigh reflected discouragement. "It's pretty tough to prey on little girls in the woods nowadays.

They're all taking karate, and their grandmothers live in condos. And wool gives me a rash.''

"Another illusion shattered," Erin protested. "I thought you were the biggest, baddest wolf in three states."

"I don't mind being 'big' and 'bad,' but the lone wolf role is wearing thin," he noted. He slipped his hand under her pullover to warm it against her skin. "I sure wouldn't mind denning up with a pretty little she-wolf, if I could find one with green eyes and soft yellow hair." He kissed the top of her head and added, "I've always been partial to green eyes."

"Hard to find in a wolf."

"Hard to find in a *woman*. It's more than color." He stroked the curve of her waist in a gesture that was soothing to both of them. "I think it's that certain emerald sparkle you flash at me when you suddenly realize I've been putting you on."

"Which sometimes takes me a while."

"Or it's that sultry jade look, the one that says to me, 'Honey, you ain't seen *nuthin'* yet.' "

"Do I have a look that says that?" she wondered innocently.

"You bet you do, and I'm beginning to think it must be true."

"Mmm, good. That gives you something to look forward to." Her hand toyed with the big oval belt buckle that lay on his stomach, comfortably unfastened. "Tell me more about this denning up. Assuming I'm the female with the right criteria, what does it entail?"

"Mating for life," he whispered.

"Is that all?"

"If you agree to that, the rest can be worked out. If you wanted children..."

"Oh, Hunter, I've dreamed of a child," she said quickly. Her voice was becoming husky. "But the child I've dreamed of has always been yours."

"The male wolf helps in raising the cubs," he told her. It was a dream he'd had, too, and he knew what part he wanted to play. "Is that why you've had no children, Erin?" Her belly quivered under his hand. "Have you been waiting for me to plant my seed inside you?"

"There've been times—" they flashed through her mind—private, well-guarded moments permitted only in dark solitude "—when I've allowed myself the hope."

"If I'd known that I could have ridden up on that porch stone sober." He rolled his head back and forth in the hay. "All that time wasted."

"Maybe it wasn't entirely wasted," she said, smoothing the shirt over his chest with firmly pressing fingertips. "There won't be any question in my mind about where my happiness lies. I answered that for myself the hard way, and I value it all the more for having been given a second chance."

"I'm not going to lose you again," he promised. "We're getting married, and then we're denning up." The thought made him smile, and he was certain the stars flickering overhead were actually applauding.

Erin squeezed her eyes shut and drew a deep breath, hoping to stave off the tears that burned in her throat. The rush of air made the burning even worse, but this was no time to cry. After another steadying breath she managed to ask, "When?"

"As soon as this other thing is settled," he replied quietly.

"How can you settle it without..." Erin swallowed and tried again. "What if he... I mean, I think the man is crazy, Hunter. I don't understand why Johnny listens to him."

"Johnny has a cause, and so does Morales. It may not be the same cause, but Morales is speaking Johnny's language, and I'm not. Johnny doesn't even hear me."

"But Johnny knows you're sympathetic," Erin supplied.

"Johnny needs more than sympathy. Ray Two Bows was the mastermind of Crimson Eagle, and now he's out of the picture. The leadership fell to Johnny by default, and Morales is right there with all the answers."

"Is he preaching violence?"

Hunter sighed. "I don't know what he's preaching. I only know I can't talk to John anymore, and I'm not privy to anything that's going on down there."

"But you are sympathetic, aren't you?"

He was quiet for a moment. It was a question with a hundred answers. "I'm an Indian," he said finally. "Born and raised on the reservation. Of course I'm sympathetic. But I left the reservation to become a newspaperman, and the world's been looking different to me ever since."

"Different how?" she wondered.

"Bigger. It used to extend from horizon to horizon—Indian land as far as the eye could see, practically flat and practically empty. I can't look around me now without thinking what a tiny piece of the world this is and what a small portion of the population we are. In good times we catch the nation's fancy, but in bad times..." The observation was punctuated with a little click of his tongue. "In bad times we have a way of disappearing into the woodwork."

Erin made a silent promise to herself that if he was going into the woodwork, she was going right in with him. On second thought, she couldn't picture Hunter disappearing into any woodwork. His vision was bigger than Johnny Parker's. Sliding a hand up to his shoulder, Erin felt his frustration in the tension in his muscles. He turned to her, pushed her hair back at her temple and lifted her chin.

"You know what it feels like to be an outsider here, don't you?" he asked. She nodded, her cheek brushing against his palm. "Being on the outside looking in is part of my job, but it's different somehow when you belonged once and now you don't. Lately I've wondered whether it's worth it. Is what I'm doing really going to make a difference to anyone around here?"

"You've seen changes," she reminded him. "Your eyes light up when you talk about them."

"Yeah, I've seen some. I make a little headway with the Tribe, and then some fanatic shoots at me through the windows and sets my office on fire. Tonight he nearly—" He bit off the words, pulling Erin into his arms. "I'm not going to lose you, babe. I've got a good job in L.A. whenever I want it. Will you go with me if I decide to sell the whole works and head west?"

Pulling back from him wasn't easy, but she wanted to see his face, and she wanted him to see hers. She saw only light and shadow and the outline of the curve of a jaw set in stone. "I'll be your wife, Hunter. I'll live anywhere in the world with you, and that includes the house standing next to Brave Wolf Publishing.'' She felt his breath catch in his chest, and she smiled. ''I'm proud of what you've built here, too.''

''And I'm proud of what you're doing.'' It was an admission he'd meant to make to her before this, but there had been another kind of pride in the way. ''You and Marlys make a good team, and you've got a good thing going. If you invite all the skeptics over for crow dinner, I'll be the first one there.''

Erin laughed and squeezed him hard. ''Oh, Hunter, you have no idea how much I love you for saying that!''

''Kiss me and maybe I'll get the picture.''

Her kiss ran the gamut from gratitude to hunger in short order. He met her hunger and matched it, trading nibbles before he pushed her back against the hay and consumed her mouth with his. It was a kiss that left them both short of breath and churning inside.

''Mmm, is that how much?'' he groaned a little shakily as he lifted his head.

''Much more,'' she whispered. ''How much time have I got to make my point?''

''You know how embarrassing it's going to be if we're still out here after the sun comes up?'' Her answer was a girlish giggle. ''I have to go, Erin.''

The moment suddenly became solemn, their arms tightening around each other in protest. Judgment intruded, and they drew apart, straightening their clothes and hair as they sat up.

''You could come to see me,'' she suggested. ''I'm sure he won't—''

"No." He offered a gentle smile as he plucked a piece of straw from her hair, thinking how close they were in color, the straw and the clinging strands of cornsilk hair. He pocketed the straw before he tucked his shirt into his jeans and buckled his belt. "We can't be sure of anything right now, and I'm not going to risk leading him up here. We're going to turn Gambler out in the pasture, and you're going to be busy with the center while I get this other thing taken care of."

"This other thing! Hunter, you make it sound like a leaky faucet or something. This man is *dangerous*. The police should be the ones to—"

"The police should be the ones?" He laughed as he chucked her under the chin. "What happened to my amateur detective?" Tapping one finger on the point of her chin, he quickly added, "Forget I asked that. The police *will* be the ones. I have some pieces; Sam has some pieces. We'll put them together and close the gap between here and L.A." She looked skeptical. "Hey, I'm not going after this guy myself," he assured her. "All I do is observe and report."

"People have gotten killed for less," she reminded him quietly, glancing away.

With his hand he turned her face back to him, and when he had her full attention he smiled, taking another piece of straw from her hair. "I won't," he said simply.

"You'll call me?"

"Yes."

"I'll expect to hear from you every day."

"Then you'll have to stay put so I can get hold of you here."

"I will."

They couldn't get enough of looking at each other, since they didn't know how long it would be before they would have the chance again. The walk back to Erin's door came only shortly before the sky began to brighten.

As he had told Erin, Hunter had no intention of going after Morales. Once the next issue of the paper was out he expected Morales to come after him. His editorial was guaranteed to fan the flames in Morales's revolutionary soul. Morales's fifth column efforts would not stand up to Hunter's *Plaintalker*, which was a growing influence in the community now. If the Crimson Eagle statement got lost in the onslaught, so be it. Morales was a clear and present danger, while Crimson Eagle was a fading cry in the wilderness.

"I've got the pictures you sent." The voice at the other end of the telephone was Sam Whiteman's. "Rick Morales's photo is in my scrapbook, too, but we call him Salvadore Santana. He's with the Liberators. I could turn this over to the Bureau right now."

Hunter sucked on the end of a piece of straw he'd taken from the pocket of his denim jacket. Narrowing his eyes, he considered the block letters he'd just arranged in close order on a white paper towel: SALVADORE SANTANA. What would the FBI be likely to do at Crimson Eagle? "I don't want to cause a shootout up there, Sam. I want to figure a way to draw him out."

"You've done that twice, my friend," Sam reminded grimly. "How are your arms?"

"I'll have some scars to remind me to let the place burn next time. What do you know about this Santana?"

"He's been slippery. We think he was in on the Hernandez kidnapping, but the two we pinned it on claimed all the credit, and Santana disappeared."

With his tongue Hunter rolled the straw to the side of his mouth as he lifted a stoneware mug for a sip of black coffee. He remembered the incident. Eighteen months earlier a naturalized American citizen, Dr. Hernandez, had been abducted, brutally murdered and left in a drainage ditch, ending an old dispute he'd had with Liberator politics.

"Johnny Parker can't handle it, Sam. He's lost his perspective. He'd make a foolhardy attempt to protect this guy, and people would get hurt. I need your help."

"I need some time to tie up a case here," Sam said. "Can you sit tight and give me a few days?"

"When the paper comes out, that editorial comes out with it," Hunter responded.

"When will that be?"

"Friday."

"I'll be there."

After he hung up Hunter leaned on the kitchen counter on his elbows and studied the name. Rick Morales was a vandal. Salvadore Santana was a cold-blooded killer. Hunter remembered the look on Erin's face when he'd opened the van's back doors. He imagined Morales opening those doors and Erin waiting for him, clutching the tire iron in her hands. Shaking the image from his brain, he sloshed his coffee, and a dark pool stained the white counter top.

Hunter wiped it up with the paper bearing the name
SALVADORE SANTANA.

"I know it's late, Erin. I didn't wake you up, did
I?"

His voice sounded especially good in the dark. Erin
settled back on the pillow and held the receiver close
against her ear. "Not exactly."

"Where are you?"

"In bed. But I'm not asleep."

"And I'm not going to apologize for that. I needed
to hear your voice. I was just...thinking about you."
Hunter slid a package of cigarettes across the counter,
just out of his reach. All he wanted was one, and he
flicked the ash from that one into the ashtray before
dragging on it again.

"You're not smoking again, are you?"

"Not exactly." How did she know?

"If it helps, I might try it."

"Don't bother. It doesn't." He stuck the cigarette
in the corner of his mouth and reached between his
legs to pull the counter stool under him. "Talk to me,
Erin. Tell me what you're wearing."

"A nightgown."

"What color?"

"Green, I think. I'm lying here in the dark. Wait a
minute, I'll..."

"No. Don't turn the light on. Keep it dark and pretend I'm there with you."

Something deep in her stomach twisted into a tight
knot, and it hurt. "It's not the same," she whispered.
"You can't touch me, and I want you to touch me,
Hunter. It's been—"

"Two weeks. I know. I'll be there soon."

"Will you ride right up on the porch?"

"And make a fool of myself over you?" He chuckled, warming her. "Of course."

Eyes closed, she put her hand over her belly and imagined his hand there. "Where are you, Hunter?"

"In the kitchen. I was in bed, but I came in here for—" he looked at the object distastefully "—a cigarette." He snatched the ashtray from across the counter and stubbed the cigarette out.

"What are you wearing?"

"Jeans."

"Is that all?"

"Yes."

"When Bernie came over that time you were just wearing jeans, and I wanted to throw a blanket over you," she remembered. "You're very sexy in jeans. I like the way you wear them."

"They're getting tighter by the minute."

"If I were there with you I could—"

"I know you could," he said tightly. "I miss you so much, I hurt with it, Erin."

"Don't," she pleaded, her eyes burning. Then an idea popped into her head, and she shoved the bittersweet moment aside. "Hunter, you could take some time off. We could go somewhere—anywhere—and let somebody else take care of all this. Tell the police all you know. They'll haul Morales in and hold him for a while, get in touch with Interpol or something. He's bound to be wanted."

"You've seen too many movies." He hadn't told her about his recent conversations with Sam. She didn't have to know that he was sitting on a powder keg.

She'd probably try to elbow him over and hop up there, too. "I've talked with a policeman. When the time is right they'll move in. Meanwhile I've got to be here, and you've got to stay right where you are so I can call you when I can't get to sleep."

She sighed. "Am I better than cigarettes?"

"No comparison."

"Even over the phone?"

"Your voice is a caress in itself." He chuckled. "Unfortunately."

Smiling, she lowered her voice as she spoke into the receiver. "Honey, you ain't seen *nuthin'* yet."

He grinned. "Neither have you. Try to go back to sleep with that in mind."

There was a moment's silence and then, "Hunter?"

"Hmm?"

"I'm sorry for making your jeans too tight."

"No problem."

The Morales situation had become a chess match, and Hunter had made the most recent move. The paper came out on Friday. Hunter knew that Morales hadn't missed the pointed questions he'd posed for "Johnny Parker's top adviser at Crimson Eagle." Who was he, and what was his interest in the Lakota Sioux? Sam had been delayed, but he would be there in a day or two. Hunter hoped Morales's response would wait a day or two, as well.

The phone in Hunter's office rang differently Saturday night. He reached for it, then hesitated, the skin crawling on the back of his neck as he allowed a second shrill ring. He knew this wasn't the call he wanted.

Something told him this call would shake his nerve to the core.

"Brave Wolf?"

The voice was muffled, unidentifiable, inhuman.

"Yes, this is Brave Wolf."

"Listen."

There was some shuffling at the other end of the line, then a delicate groan. Hunter gripped the phone, waiting."Hunter? I'm all right. I don't want you to—"

"Erin?" There was another groan and more shuffling. "Erin! Where are you?"

"She is with Johnny Parker's top adviser."

The low growl that came from Hunter's throat had nothing to do with the wild fear that shot through his body. It had to do with the terrible urge that came with the fear—the urge to strike back. "I'll kill you if you hurt her, Morales. I'll find you in hell, and I'll kill you."

"I was depending on your sentimentality, Brave Wolf. Your woman is very stubborn. I think she wants to protect you, which is foolish, of course. You have five seconds to advise her to be cooperative."

Hunter swallowed, searching for a calm tone of voice. "Erin, do exactly as they say. Don't do anything crazy. I won't let them hurt you, I promise."

"Now *you* will do exactly as I say," the muffled voice continued. "If you have trouble following directions, I assure you I will not find it difficult to cut this pretty lady's throat."

# Chapter 12

The call had come in the early evening. Erin had been in the middle of eating a tuna sandwich and a fruit plate. She picked up the phone in the kitchen, eyeing the *Plaintalker*, which lay on the counter with a stack of unopened mail. She'd get to that after supper.

"Is this Erin O'Neill?"

"Yes, it is."

"Uhh—listen, I just left a guy sittin' on the road down there by Rattlesnake Butte. You know where that is?" The voice drawled a bit and sounded far away.

Erin wondered what some man sitting on the road could possibly have to do with her, but she answered, "Yes, I know where that is."

"Well, his car broke down, see—little white foreign job—and he give me this number and asked me to call you, tell you to come pick him up. Name of Brave Wolf."

"Hunter?"

"Yeah, that's him. I generally don't pick people up, specially off them back roads, and a guy don't wanna leave his car out there, anyway. You might wanna hurry. He's been sittin' down there quite a while now."

"Yes, I will. How far from Rattlesnake Butte?"

"Right up there past the curve around the butte. You can't miss it. Car's sittin' right there alongside the road."

"Thank you for taking the time to call, Mr.—"

"No trouble. Take it easy, now." Click.

Erin smiled. It wasn't much more than a ten-minute drive to Rattlesnake Butte, but the road was a tire killer, among other things. More people broke down on that stretch of ruts and washboard than in the rest of the whole country. And, at that moment, Hunter was sitting up there stewing. God, it would be great to coax a smile out of him again!

The big, square-topped butte was a landmark in the area. It was said that a huge, flat rock housed a great rattlesnake den at the top of the butte, but Erin had twice declined Hunter's invitation to hike up there and see for herself. He'd also promised a panoramic view, but that hadn't been enough enticement to overcome the threat of rattlesnakes.

At dusk the butte loomed magnificently against the streaked red-and-blue sky. The gravel road wound around its base, rising above the rolling pastures for a good view of late summer's fading greens, darkened now with waning light. As she rounded the curve Erin saw the small white car parked on the shoulder of the road. It looked empty. He'd probably climbed the butte to watch the sunset. Erin secured her parking brake and thought about the snakes. She pictured Hunter standing on a flat rock high above the world, a breeze ruffling his thick, black hair, and her insides liquefied. What the heck, she'd dodge the snakes.

She peered through the window and saw no one in either the front or the back. Straightening slowly, she frowned. A second glance through the window confirmed the feeling that something was wrong. This was the wrong car, though in this light it looked very much like Hunter's. Quickly glancing right and left, she started back toward her own car, then whirled to face the sound at her back.

A dark figure sprang from the ditch on the low side of the road. Erin managed three steps before she was jerked off her feet, her breath knocked away by the arm that crushed her around the middle.

"Do not struggle," the man whispered in her ear. "You may hurt yourself, and then your man will be angry with me. I want only to reason with him."

Erin tipped her head back and shrieked at the sky, but like everything else in the area, it was too distant to hear her. She might as well have been on a desert island. Her captor's laughter underscored that fact as she tried to squirm out of his grasp.

"I suspect you would not be good company on the little drive we're going to take, Miss O'Neill." Erin watched with horror as the man inserted a key in the lock of the car's trunk. Throwing all her strength into the effort, she pushed at the steely arm that held her, craning her neck at the same moment to get a look at the man's face. She knew, of course, that she would see the same lean face she'd confronted by firelight at Crimson Eagle—the face of Rick Morales.

"What are you going to do with me?" she demanded.

"It will be best for both of us if you ride back here," he said, his voice betraying no emotion as he raised the lid of the trunk. "This way you will not make me angry, and I will not be tempted to injure you. It should not be necessary for me to do you any harm before we meet with your man."

"Hunter's done nothing to you," Erin protested. "There's no call for any of this. You must be—"

Erin's words were cut off as Morales pushed her head and shoulders into the trunk. Bent double over the bumper, she still struggled to get out, but her efforts were futile.

"The trunk is not airtight, Miss O'Neill, but I would not advise too much exertion on your part. Shallow breathing will serve you well." With that he shut her off from the world.

Erin felt the claws of panic digging into the back of her neck. She curled herself up into a tight little ball and shut her eyes against the darkness. Total darkness. Cramped quarters. Little air. A madman at the wheel. Oh, God. Dear God! These were the things she must put out of her mind. She told herself to think of Hunter. No, this man wanted to harm Hunter; she mustn't think about that. She must think about something else, something neutral. She must plan for tomorrow. Tomorrow she had an appointment with Carol Walks Alone. Carol was . . . Carol had some designs for handmade skirts. Picture the skirts, Erin, she thought. Picture the skirts and take small breaths.

Hunter had been directed to a phone booth in a town twenty-five miles south of McLaughlin. There he received another call and directions to return to Brave Wolf Publishing. Morales/Santana had refused to put Erin on the phone again. A wild-goose chase, Hunter thought as he gripped the steering wheel in both hands and bore down on the road as though he would have his tires leave an angry impression.

Santana could run him up and down the road all night. All the while, he had Erin. At *this moment* he had her. What would he do to her? *What would that scum do to Erin?* The whine of radial tires against pavement filled Hunter's ears like a distant scream. She was scared, as he was. Her heart was pounding, just as his was. Santana was hurting her. Oh, God, he *knew* Santana was hurting her! The painful knot in Hunter's stomach tightened.

Brave Wolf Publishing was dark. Hunter didn't remember turning the lights out, but he must have. He knew he hadn't locked the door, and, sure enough, the knob turned readily in his hand. Instinct guided him to the office door, which he found closed. Strange, he thought. He was sure he'd been in too much of a hurry to close the door behind him. He opened it cautiously and flicked the light switch on the wall. Erin was the first thing he saw, sitting behind his desk.

She squinted against the light. Oh, God, it was Hunter! She gripped the arms of the chair and struggled to focus on him. Not daring to speak, she flicked her eyes quickly to the right. Hunter's eyes followed hers to the corner of the office, to the dark-eyed figure leaning against a file cabinet, and then to the weapon in his hand. The handgun was aimed at Erin's head.

"Come in, Brave Wolf." Salvadore Santana's smile was small and sinister, revealing only the cutting edge of a row of stained teeth. "You do move quickly. I appreciate that, because I would like to conclude my business with you quickly."

As he took a step inside the door Hunter returned his attention to the terrified woman sitting behind the desk. He hurriedly searched for visible evidence of harm done to her, but he found none. He flashed a murderous gaze back at Santana. "If your business is with me, then let her go," Hunter growled.

"I think you will behave much better in the presence of a lady," Santana predicted. His black eyes glittered. "She is the kind of woman a man wants to impress. In the short time we have spent together I think I have made a lasting impression on her myself. Isn't that so, Miss O'Neill?"

Erin glanced fearfully at the man with the gun. His expression of triumph made her glance away.

"Erin, are you... hurt?" The words scratched inside Hunter's throat. A quick shake of her head did nothing to reassure him.

Santana laughed. "I would have good use for a woman like this. She is able to follow instructions, you see. She has been told not to say a word."

"What have you done to her?" Hunter demanded.

"I have used her to bring you here. You have your way of getting people's attention. This is mine."

"You have my attention," Hunter insisted quietly. "Let her go, and I'm all ears."

A sputtering chuckle preceded Santana's response. "All ears! Another amusing American expression. I will file it away for future use. Miss O'Neill will tell you that I can do a very convincing Midwestern American over the telephone." He composed himself, taking a step toward Erin. "Your problem, Brave Wolf, is that you are too much an American and not enough a native."

Without thought Hunter took a step closer to the desk. "I don't see how any problem I might have affects you, Santana."

The strange name brought a furrow to Erin's brow, but both men ignored her confusion.

"It affects me because obviously you have contacts in Los Angeles, and you have made use of them on behalf of the CIA. A true native American knows that the CIA is the enemy."

"I have no contacts with the CIA," Hunter told him. "I know somebody with the L.A.P.D. That's hardly federal. All I wanted to know was who you really were."

Santana smiled. "You still don't know who I *really* am. Your ears cannot hear me. Your eyes cannot see me. You are not one of us."

"Who's *us*, Santana? I'm Lakota, and I'm also a U.S. citizen," Hunter said, edging toward the desk. "Who the hell are you?"

"Stay where you are." Santana hooked a hand underneath Erin's chin and brought her head up, laying the barrel of the handgun against her temple. Erin closed her eyes, and Hunter's breath caught in his throat. "I am the man who has a loaded pistol pointed at your woman's head. Would you have me angry?"

"No," Hunter said evenly.

"Would you want to make me squeeze this hand into a tight fist?" Eyes ablaze, Hunter shook his head. "I thought not. She is lovely. She is very soft and sweet smelling, is she not?" Hunter simply stared at Erin, whose eyes and lips were shut tight, the latter quivering only slightly. "Answer me!"

"Yes, she is," Hunter whispered.

"You would not want her to be touched by any other man," Santana supposed.

"No, I would not."

"I thought not. That is why I thought you would want her to die with you. It will be very dramatic, Brave Wolf. You will both go up in flames with your precious newspaper. It will appeal to your sentimentality, and—" he offered a sardonic smile "—it will make all the newspapers."

"Johnny Parker will finally know who you are, Santana."

"It doesn't matter anymore," Santana said with a shrug. "The Crimson Eagle movement has stalled. Parker is no longer useful."

"Do you plan to kill him, too?" Hunter asked. "Or have you done that already?"

"Of course not. Parker is a harmless man. He may even be able to serve again."

"Not if you kill me."

Santana smiled slowly, the smug expression almost as infuriating to Hunter as the sound of the man's voice. "You would be surprised what a man can be made to believe and to discount, especially a man who is driven by fear."

Forget the oily smile, Hunter told himself. Forget the cocky lilt in his voice. Keep him talking. Stay eye to eye. Don't lose him. "And Johnny was afraid to make any decisions on his own," Hunter offered.

"Parker was afraid to make mistakes. He was afraid of failure. He wanted guidance, and I gave it to him."

With a subtle shift of his weight Hunter gained another inch. The man wanted to talk. He wanted to make his cause known, even to someone he counted as good as dead. Feed into his ego, Hunter thought. Keep the conversation going. "Crimson Eagle was conceived as a peaceful protest. That hardly seems your style."

"There is no such thing as a *peaceful* protest." Santana spat out the word "peaceful" as though it were blasphemous. "How can an intelligent man be so completely blind? Are you unaware of what is happening in this hemisphere, Brave Wolf? The native people will speak with one voice, and we will be heard. Oppression is not a peaceful thing, and it cannot be countered with your sit-ins and your—"

"You killed a woman who had nothing to do with oppression, Santana. You murdered a woman who was a friend to the Lakota people."

"The movement needed a bombshell," Santana explained. "It needed to smell blood. It needed to be decried by the public so that it would tighten its ranks."

The confession penetrated the fog of fear in Erin's brain. This man had killed her sister simply to stir up trouble. She glanced at Hunter, but his gaze was fixed on Morales, or Santana—whoever he was. Something in Hunter's eyes told her not to distract him.

They were the eyes of a stalker who had cornered his prey. The weapon was in Santana's hand, but the control was in Hunter's eyes. She noticed his subtle inching forward, but Santana did not.

"Is it time for another bombshell, Santana? Is that why you're here?" From Hunter's tone he could as well have been asking whether it was time for supper.

"There is anger here," Santana said thoughtfully. "And anger is the seed of revolution. But you do not speak for the people, Brave Wolf. You tell them things they do not need to know, and you confuse them."

"I don't deal in propaganda. I observe and report." The line was becoming a catch phrase for him, he realized. He said it automatically. "Whether they need to know about it or not, the people will hear about my sudden death, and *that* will confuse them."

"They will be angry, and many accusations will be made. You might even become a martyr, Brave Wolf. Who knows? You made a mistake when you questioned my presence publicly, but I may find a way to make you one of the movement's fallen heroes. It is surprising how useful a corpse can be."

The barrel of Santana's gun had strayed from Erin's temple. Hunter's penetrating gaze had not flickered, but he knew. His hand would have to be quicker than Santana's eye. Reflexes honed in the rodeo arena had not been allowed to deteriorate over the years, and Hunter had the patience of an Indian. Before he acted the time...must...be...

A door squeaked. Santana's eyes widened as he lifted his head toward the sound, the belated awareness of the trapped prey.

Hunter hurled himself at the arm holding the gun. It was the quick, fluid move of a predator, every muscle suddenly called into play. Erin jumped away from the colliding bodies, catching herself after two stumbling steps. She turned just in time to watch Hunter dash Santana's arm once, twice, against the file cabinet. The gun sailed from the man's hand, hit the carpeted floor with a heavy thud and bounced across the threshold into the outer office area. A feminine hand retrieved it and brought it to the door, dangling it carefully from neatly manicured fingertips.

"Hunter, did you lose your—" wide-eyed, Bernie looked back and forth between Erin and the struggling men "—gun? What in the ... ?"

Erin took the gun from Bernie's hand and swung it toward Santana like a practiced marksman. Hunter had him by the hair, had his chin hooked over the top of the filing cabinet, one arm twisted high over his back. The man gurgled as Hunter pushed his throat over the corner of the cabinet, effectively cutting off his wind. By the way it dangled awkwardly from his elbow, the other arm appeared to have been broken.

"I have the gun, Hunter," Erin said quietly. Hunter didn't seem to hear. He had become a body of savage pressure, and his prey gasped pathetically under the strain. "Hunter, let him go!" Erin pleaded. "You'll kill him!"

Hunter turned his head toward the sound of her voice, and the blazing hatred in his eyes waned visibly when he saw her. One muscle at a time his body relaxed, allowing Santana a few noisy gulps of air. "Are you all right?" Hunter managed, searching her eyes for the damage he feared.

"He didn't hurt me," she assured him. "He didn't."

Santana suddenly became a slimy thing, and Hunter drew back, loath to touch him any longer. Santana slithered down the cabinet that had become his only support and dropped to the floor in a heap. It was Erin who sighed with relief as she handed Hunter the gun.

"I saw the light," Bernie began excitedly. "I thought it was awfully late for you to be working. Did this guy break in here?"

"Call the police, Bernie," Hunter said, still fighting the urge to crush the breath out of the malignancy on the floor. "This man is a murderer."

While they waited for the police Bernie asked question after question. Hunter's responses were clipped, his attention on the man who sat on the floor, his broken arm cradled in his lap. Erin sat quietly, her mind struggling to make the shift from terror to tranquillity.

A little while later, as he sat on the edge of his desk with his arms folded over his chest, Hunter gave his statement to the police. Santana had already been taken away. When Hunter had finished he listened to Erin tell of the phone call, the trap Santana had set for her and the ride in the trunk of a car. She sat with her hands folded tightly in her lap, and she rarely lifted her eyes as she talked. Hunter clenched his teeth until he could take it no longer.

"It's been a tough night, Joe. We can take care of the rest of this later." Joe Tiger turned a questioning look toward Hunter, who jerked his chin toward the door. With a nod Joe mumbled some words of apology and took his leave.

They sat apart until they heard the door close. Erin stared at her hands, her hair falling in a tangled mass around her face. That disarray, more than anything else, made her seem more vulnerable than she ever had before. Hunter went to her, dropped one knee beside her chair and took her face in both his hands. "It's all right now," he said, his voice low and soft. "You're all right."

Her eyes swam, struggling to fill themselves with him. Nodding, her lips pursed stubbornly against a sob, she stretched her arm toward his neck and slid off the chair as he gathered her into his lap. She crooned his name in a tearful litany as he held her close and rocked her, swallowing his own grateful tears.

"Let's go home," Hunter whispered when the tears were spent at last. Erin nodded, sniffling.

"Here, use my sleeve. Cowboys don't carry handkerchiefs," he offered.

Erin glanced into his tender, teasing eyes and laughed, swiping at the wetness on her cheeks with the back of her hand. "I thought they carried big red bandannas."

"I keep those in a drawer by my bed. We'll go get you one." He helped her to her feet and led her from the building, all the while keeping her close. From the time he'd heard her terrified voice on the phone until the moment he'd knocked the gun from Santana's hand, he had cursed every curse and promised every promise he could think of in the hope that heaven would protect his woman. From now on, he swore, he would keep her close, keep her safe.

Erin took a deep breath of cool night air. It smelled clean. It felt good on her damp cheeks. She'd probably have trouble with small, dark places for some time to come, she thought, remembering the terrible noise of the muffler beneath her head and the feeling that she'd already used every available molecule of oxygen.

At the house Hunter let Blondie in from the backyard and locked the back door as usual, then he paused for a moment's consideration, laying his hands on Erin's shoulders. "Can I get you anything before I make love to you?"

"No." Her eyes said that the latter was all she wanted.

"Tomorrow we'll collect your belongings from the mission. The wedding is up to you. Just say the word and I'll be there. But from tonight until forever, you come home to me."

"And you'll come home to me," she whispered, then met his kiss with the eagerness of hers.

Without any more words they went to his bedroom, where he undressed her by the light of a small table lamp. Beneath her blouse and slacks he found purple bruises on the delicate fabric of her skin, and he kissed them—on the inside of her arm, on her shoulder, beneath her breast, on her hip. The eyes he finally raised to hers were soft with the pain his lips had just tasted.

"At first I refused to speak to you on the phone," she explained quietly. "I knew you'd come, and I knew he wanted to hurt you. I didn't want to help him trap you."

"What did he do?"

"Nothing very terrible." She lifted a bare shoulder in sad dismissal, wishing she could say she'd withstood some unspeakable torment for him. She hadn't. She'd been too scared. "I gave in before he did anything very terrible." The little smile she offered was an apology. "I've decided not to take out a detective's license. A little twist on the arm and I can't spill the beans fast enough."

His eyes still weren't satisfied. Was she holding anything back from him? Was she hoping to spare him something she wasn't able to spare herself? She took his smooth cheeks in her hands and plumbed the depth of his troubled eyes with hers. "I'm fine, Hunter. The only damage he did is just what you see. I wish I hadn't been so stupid—falling for that silly story of his and then—"

He pulled her into his arms with a ragged sigh. "Oh, God, Erin, you're apologizing for not protecting me. You should be raking me over the coals. *I'm* the one who should have protected *you* from all this."

"Why?"

"Because I'm the man," he groaned.

"And I'm the woman," she whispered into the thick thatch of hair behind his ear. "It works out nicely, doesn't it?"

"Yeah." He drew back to offer her a gentle smile. "And it'll work out even better once I get you out of this godforsaken place and get you settled in a heavily mortgaged house with a sensible brown station wagon in the garage."

"Hunter..."

"Roses in the front yard and a couple of kids in the back. In fact—" his belt buckle rattled, and then a snap clicked "—I wouldn't mind getting started on one of those right now."

"Mmm." The hand on her breast made her forget her objections. "Front yard or back?" she whispered, sinking beneath him to the mattress.

"You can plant the roses, honey. I get to plant the kids."

# Chapter 13

Johnny Parker read the words above the door once again. Brave Wolf Publishing. This was the business Hunter had built from the ground up—the business Rick Morales would have burned to the ground with Hunter and Erin inside it if Hunter had given him the chance. Johnny owed Hunter an apology. Hell, he owed his friend much more than that, but there was no way to make proper amends for the trouble he'd helped to cause. Facing Hunter would be one of the most difficult things he'd ever had to do.

After dragging himself out of his old brown pickup Johnny headed for the building, stopping to examine a dent in the side of Hunter's van as he passed it. He hadn't seen that there when they'd had the van up at Crimson Eagle. He always noticed things like that. He'd been a pretty good auto-body man in his day,

and it was high time he got back to it. Maybe someday he'd have his own business, too.

There was no one at the front desk, and Johnny realized that it was probably after five. He never wore a
watch anymore, but he figured he'd get one soon.
Surveying the empty chairs and abandoned desks behind the reception area, he wondered why the door
was unlocked if the place was closed.

"Forget something, Bernie?"

Johnny turned his head in the direction of Hunter's voice. A nearby door stood ajar. Johnny heard a
whisper and then a feminine giggle, and he knew he'd
interrupted something. He turned to leave.

"Johnny!" Johnny cocked his chin back over his
shoulder. There was Hunter grinning at him from the
doorway of his office. "What are you doing? Spying
on me again?"

Johnny swallowed, shoving his hands in his pockets as he turned back toward the man he'd admired all
his life. He didn't blame Hunter for believing what he
did about him. Maybe he'd never be able to make
things right between them. Who'd ever believe a man
could work so closely, *live* so closely, with someone
and know nothing of who he really was?

"Is that Johnny Parker *again*?" The voice was Erin's, full of pink smiles and green-eyed delight. "If
that boy isn't following us on horseback, he's hiding
behind the haystack. Can't he find a girl of his own?"

"It isn't that he can't find one, honey. It's just that
he doesn't know what to do with her." Hunter's easy
grin made Johnny relax a little. He returned the smile
when Erin appeared in the doorway, too, slipping under Hunter's arm. "I swear there's radar in that beak

of his," Hunter teased. "I get you all puckered up for a kiss, and he's right there taking notes."

"I've still got a lot to learn," Johnny said, shuffling a little reluctantly in his friends' direction. "And you always had such great style."

"Well, I like to keep in shape, John," Hunter quipped into the imaginary microphone his fist made. "I get in as much practice as I can. My partner and I were just practicing for the big one, as a matter of fact."

"The big one?"

"That's right, John," Hunter's pseudoofficial broadcasting voice replied. "The big wedding kiss. With a whole churchful of people looking on, my reputation will be on the line. I intend to bow out of circulation with a flourish."

Johnny grinned. "Congratulations. It's about time."

"We think so, too," Hunter said, reaching for the hand Johnny offered him.

"Hunter, I'm sorry about Morales," Johnny said quietly. He stared at their clasped hands and took a deep breath. "I guess...I wanted you to be wrong about him, so I listened to a stranger and turned my back on a friend."

Johnny's hand slid away. "You thought I turned my back on you when I couldn't be any more help to you at Crimson Eagle," Hunter said, laying a brotherly hand on Johnny's shoulder. "And, in a way, maybe I did."

Johnny looked up, surprised. "You never turned your back on me, Hunter. I just didn't understand why you weren't more involved. Morales said it was because you'd sold out, and I believed him. But you aren't for sale. I know that now."

"I've got nothing to sell, John." Hunter smiled, giving the slighter man's shoulder a little shake. "I'm just a newspaperman. And I've just about decided I've got to go somewhere else to ply my trade. People say you can't go home again, and I think maybe they're right."

"What do you mean—go somewhere else?" Johnny demanded, his brows drawing down in a frown. "What about all this? You just got it started!" He glanced at Erin, and she lowered her eyes. So that was it, Johnny thought.

"It's my decision," Hunter said. "I'm too close here. I can't do what needs to be done unless people accept me on my terms."

"What terms are those?" Johnny asked.

"That I be allowed to observe and report," Hunter said with a shrug. "I must say it at least a dozen times a day, but I don't think anybody around here listens. You come to my home, I'm your cousin." He drew a circle in the air. "Yours and half the reservation's. I'll lend you my car, my best suit, whatever I've got in my billfold. But in this office I've got no relatives." The thumb he jerked over his shoulder indicated the room at his back. "On a story, I'm nobody's *cinks*."

Erin registered the Lakota word for "son," and she knew that, in the fabric of Hunter's culture, family ties were the warp and weft. For days she'd watched him struggle with this decision, and she knew there was nothing she could do to make it easier for him. She hadn't missed his long, hard looks at the Brave Wolf

Publishing sign, and she'd waited quietly, reading his thoughts.

"I know how it is," Johnny said. "You have to listen to everybody's little gripes. You agree with one, and five others come down on your head. I guess that's why I let Morales..." He glanced away, still heartsick at the thought of what the man he'd known as Rick Morales had done.

"Forget it, John. It's all over. We're looking ahead now, and I'm just thinking maybe I oughta go back to working for somebody else for a while. What about you?"

Johnny shifted his weight a little uncomfortably from one foot to the other. "I *know* I oughta work for somebody else, but I think you should keep right on doing what you're doing, Hunter. I don't know how much longer we'll keep the camp going. Already people are saying, 'Crimson Eagle Camp? Didn't they close that up yet?' We're old news." Johnny's sigh was long and hollow. "The business with Morales will muddy the issues even more. We're only holding out because we're hoping maybe we're still a thorn in some bureaucrat's side."

As he talked, the weariness in Johnny's eyes touched Erin's heart, but a sudden spark in his dull eyes reflected his quick change to urgency. "You can't quit, Hunter," he said, latching on to Hunter's arm. "You're our voice. You're our watchdog and our conscience. The big city newspapers carry your stories and let people know we're still here. Without you..." He shook his head, refusing to make a prediction.

"What about you, John?" Hunter countered. "When it's time for those people to come down from that mountain, somebody's going to have to lead the way. Are you going back to Crimson Eagle?"

His shoulders drooping, Johnny gave Hunter the old Johnny Parker grin. "That depends on what you've got in your billfold, cousin. My gas gauge is sittin' on Empty."

Blondie scratched on the bedroom door and whined pitifully. There was no mistaking the sound of her master's voice. He was in there, his every groan pricking the dog's sensitive ears. She wanted her place at the foot of his bed. There had been too many changes around here lately—another human in the house, a new bed for Blondie in the spare room, strange new scents, strange new table scraps. Whisking her claws along the grooves she'd already established in the wood, she whined again.

"What's wrong, baby?" Hunter whispered, breathing heavily into his wife's ear. "I didn't hurt you, did I?"

Erin giggled. "That's the dog, silly. Can't you tell the difference?"

With a low chuckle he rolled to his side and pulled Erin close. "In the throes of passion, it's hard to distinguish one from the other." Again the plaintive whine was heard outside the door. "That's Blondie," he confirmed immediately. "Plain, ordinary house dog. Not to be confused with the sultry growl of the hot-blooded she-wolf who's taken over my den."

"Taken over? I've just made a few small changes."

"Not to mention taking over my bed," he added. "Hogging the covers, sprawling all over me in her sleep..."

"Complaining?"

"Not on your life," he assured her, playfully nipping at her eyebrow. "You've got a honey of a sprawl." The dog whined again, and Hunter lifted his head toward the door. "Go to bed, you jealous mutt!"

"I can't imagine worse competition," Erin groaned. "Even Bernie took it better than this."

"Bernie's got better things to do than sit by the bedroom door and whine. She's probably got Sam Whiteman doing a pretty polka down at the Dew Drop Inn right about now."

"Sam was disappointed about missing all the excitement," Erin recalled. "But I'm glad he stayed for the wedding." There was more scratching against the door, this time without the whine. "Hunter, we've got to do something about that dog. Have you seen what she's done to this door?"

"Yeah," he clucked. "Poor old gal. I can't have both of you sprawling all over me. I'll replace the door if I...*before* I sell the house."

She waited a moment before asking, "You've made up your mind, then?"

"I thought...I thought we'd *both* decided, honey." He cupped a hand over the side of her face and began to soothingly massage her forehead with his thumb. "This is no place for you, Erin. I want you to be happy. I want to give you the kind of life a woman like you should—"

"No, Hunter," she said, turning her face into his hand. "You don't have to *give* me any kind of life.

We'll build it together. For the first time in my life I've found work that needs to be done by me. By *me* because I'm good at it. I'm needed here, too. Don't tell yourself you're leaving Brave Wolf Publishing because of me. I can plant roses anywhere.''

"I can't even get grass to grow out front here," he mumbled.

"We'll bring in some compost. I know how to make things grow. Hunter...do you *want* to sell the business?"

"No."

"You've never been one to turn your back on a challenge," she reminded him quietly.

"How do you really feel about staying here?" he asked. "Will a visit back east start the doubts milling in your mind again?"

With a sigh she slid a hand around the back of his neck, lacing her fingers in an abundance of tapered hair. "I know what's important now, Hunter. Love is foremost, and I've never loved anyone but you."

Hunter considered that declaration in silence for a moment. His voice was hushed when he spoke again. "You know, I survived twelve years ago when my girl left me and ended up marrying another man. I probably even became a better man for it. But you're my wife now, and I don't think I could stand to lose you twice in one lifetime."

"Twelve years ago I loved you as a girl loves a boy," she said. "That wasn't enough."

"We had something then, Erin. You can't deny that."

She drew her hand down and brushed her fingers along the smooth trough in the middle of his chest.

"We had passion, and there hadn't been any passion in my life since until I came back to find it again with you." She touched her lips to the hard heat of his breastbone as her hand slid to his belly. "I came back to love you as a woman, Hunter. I've come full circle. I'm not running away from passion anymore, and I'm not afraid of the pain or the shortcomings or the disappointments, because I know we'll survive those things. I know because I love you as a woman loves a man." She smiled against the satin surface of his chest when he sucked his breath in. "And that's with gentle tenacity, my love."

"Is that what it's called?" Nuzzling her, he groaned. "Mmm. I love that gentle tenacity."

"Shall I start something growing out front, then?"

He gave a short, lascivious laugh. "I won't even touch that line, honey. It's too damned good the way it stands."

"I know," she whispered. "I love to grow things, and I was just thinking about the seed you wanted to plant."

"Do you think it's time?"

"I think it might take root now, Hunter."

"And if it feeds on love..."

"It can't help but grow."

\* \* \* \* \*